Homes

The Askance 2014
Short Story Collection
including all the finalists
in the 2013 competition

This book is a work of fiction. Names, characters, places and events are either the
product of the authors' imaginations or are used fictitiously. Any resemblance to
actual persons living or dead, events or locales, is entirely coincidental.

Published 2013 by Askance Publishing Cambridge

ISBN 978 1909009 158

British Library Cataloguing in Publication Data.
A catalogue record for this book is available from the British Library.

A Message from Emmaus

For many who experience homelessness, loss of self-esteem is a major obstacle they must overcome. People who live in Emmaus communities carry out meaningful work in our social enterprises, making a real contribution. As well as a stable home, Emmaus provides a purpose and the chance to make a difference.

Emmaus Cambridge is committed to working as a community, sharing a life where everyone is treated equally, and living in harmony with dignity by helping those less fortunate than ourselves.

Thanks

This year Askance decided to also hold a competition for the front cover image of this anthology in association with Cambridge International Arts, who ran the competition. We are very grateful to Cambridge School of Art for kindly donating a generous prize.

Our thanks and appreciation also goes to Fine & Country Estate Agents who were delighted to be involved and who sponsored the writing competition with another substantial prize.

Many of the entrants both for the cover and the writing competitions were motivated by the connection to homelessness and were new to entering competitions. Askance is delighted to have been able to inspire such fresh engagement. The winning image by Jane Fisher appears as the cover of this book and was selected by five artist judges for its story-telling quality, wonderful application of colour, and gentle ambiguity.

Special thank-you also to Beth Reid, Judith Rumgay and Marta Bartolik for their extra support and willingly given time.

Editor's Introduction

When Askance chose a theme as open to interpretation as 'home', it satisfied several needs: a strong link to Emmaus, the charity partner, a clear connection with the commercial sponsors Fine & Country, and as broad a canvas as possible for writers' imaginations. And what imaginations! Once again the inbox has filled with writing of astonishing quality from all corners of the globe, once again writers have found unique voices to express their own particular insight into 'home'.

Of particular satisfaction has been the response to Askance's decision to lower the age limit for entries. The result was several stories with the fresh edge of youth and we are all rewarded by seeing two new young writers, both students, published in *Homes.*

It is right to mention *The Road to Emmaus* before all others, not least because it is part story, part dream, part lyrical prose poem. It introduces the collection and has its own foreword from the publisher, and fittingly, its own cautionary advice to writers. Perhaps predictably homelessness featured in several entries, but the writing is far from predictable. *One Man's Meat* from Phil Arnold gives us a funny, revealing story of silvertails and beggars, as does MV Blake's poignant *In Judith Veritas.* Not alone amongst the stories, *Oxford Dogs* from Linda Brucesmith reflects real events and weaves a beautiful, if tragic, fiction around them. Sue Dean's *The Red Geranium* also uses the plight of the homeless, but as a destination for her highly engaging story of the slide from have to have-not.

Alex Ayling's *Search For Point Home* presents a different, youthful view of lost dreams and being homeless despite having a roof over your head, certainly a story for our times. As is *Number One Girl,* Jane Carmichael's intimate account of having a child serving in a war zone. From another age and continent comes *When Sister Came Home*, Phil Arnold's second contribution, a gentle tale of return set in the 1960s. Hugh Kellett's *Homeward* also harks back to distant days in a keenly felt story with roots in the colonial service and the repressed emotions of loss and desertion.

That loss and desertion is heart-breakingly mirrored in Dave Pescod's *Pink Leather*, a tale which will quite unsentimentally touch anyone who's ever been close to the world of care homes. Hugh Kellett's *The New Home* also has old-age at its heart but finds the pleasures of memory and imagination compensating for the more familiar ills. *A Commission* from Tim Futter looks at new and old homes, both desirable or abhorrent according to one's point of view.

The desirability of somewhere to call home, be it physical or otherwise, is the constant theme of Anne Garvey's back-breaking story of domestic service, *Edie*. A home lost despite equally hard labour comes from Jackie Hawkins in her moving *Portrait of a Farmer, With Leaves*. Hardship is the theme of Simon Humphrey's closely observed and distressing *Service Delivery*, which gives us the realities of home a world away from most of our comfortable Cambridge lives.

Despite the threatening title, Catherine E. Byfield's *Home is Where The Heart (of Darkness) Is* brings a touch of humour to a bizarre situation, as does Linden Ford perhaps more darkly in *Burrow*, where childhood fantasies leak disturbingly into adult life. *Home For Valentine's Day* draws us into another slightly unsettling world, cleverly conjured up from Hannah Constance's fertile imagination.

Abandon, Margaret Loescher's multifaceted story set in a derelict house, is as American as mom's apple pie, and is all the richer for it. From a very different standpoint, Tom Wiseman's *Where The Heart Is* embraces the physical and the spiritual, the journey and the return, in one mystical story, while the deceptively simple *24 Hours* from Zainab Thamer uses a physical journey crossing cultures and languages to demonstrate a personal one, as home changes its meaning as the miles fly by.

We all have our own ideas of home and what makes it. There are an infinite number of stories that might be written, each with its own voice, each with its own appeal. But it is difficult to imagine a collection with greater depth, broader vision or more pure gems than here in our writers' Homes.

It has again been a privilege to edit an Askance anthology and my thanks go to all the authors for their willing and good-humoured co-operation. It has also been a pleasure to be part of the judging panel. Any one of several stories could have been justly chosen without any complaint, and my own personal choice varied from day to day, not through dithering, but because of the competing claims of a number of original and well written stories. After sincere and conscientious consideration, the judges were more than happy to give their vote to *Abandon* by Margaret Loescher, a truly outstanding piece of writing, yet which only took the nod by a whisker.

DJ Wiseman
September 2013

The Stories

The Way to Emmaus: A Foreword

The Way to Emmaus is a special story for many reasons. Written by an Emmaus companion, it casts light on one man's journey through homelessness and brings the fragility of street existence to life. On first reading, I immediately felt the story needed editing and tidying up, but when I met the author I changed my mind.

The writer, once a known poetry and prose writer in his homeland insisted that I made no attempt to scrub up his grammar and clarify meaning. With little English himself, the work had been translated by his daughter, who now lived on the other side of the world. I spoke to him through a translator from his own country and on reading the story in his native tongue she proclaimed, "this is so beautiful!" He explained that *The Way to Emmaus* should be considered as a hyperactive stream of consciousness. It mattered not to him that people picked up on every nuance or paused for breath. Some of it was not even clear to him, and drawn from stories he had heard. The work appeared to me on the page as somewhere between a rant and a mumble and I quickly realised that in order for the reader to hear the writer's voice, it needed to carry its imperfections with it.

For most of us having a work published would puff our chest. Books might be bought as Christmas presents and it would certainly be worth a mention on our social media status updates and added to our CV. The writer of this story, however, has requested to remain anonymous. With the magical sparkle of a creative soul he said it would be fun if nobody knew which Emmaus companion had written the story. His modesty was moving, especially as by his own and anybody else's measure he has few possessions and claims his life "has not amounted to much." There are lessons there for us all, that I do not need to spell out.

I asked him more about how he ended up living at Emmaus. The story dances neatly around the subject. He said he owed everything to Karen at West London Day Centre and added that he would love to travel to London to present her with a big bunch of flowers, but he feared he might slide into old ways if he did that.

So with the writer's permission, I would like to dedicate not only this story, but this whole collection of stories to Karen, and for the many like her who work to support the homeless.

Caroline Jaine
Founder of Askance Publishing

The Way to Emmaus

Let me tell you about myself. It comes unusually easy to some people to tell about themselves. They pronounce their lives worthy a literary depiction. Their lives are sequences of unprecedented events, in which they play the leading parts. I would never dare to claim that my life is worthy a book. There are those of my deeds which I can hardly accept, there are the others, which I try not to remember. You may analyse them by yourselves, since I took a risk of telling you about myself, within the limits of my modest literary ability. I have been wondering if I should write in the first person or should I create a fictional character? Eventually I have decided not to entrust a fictional narrator to describe my life. Do not count on sensational scenes from the life of the homeless on the streets of London, or on their lofty rebirth in Emmaus, don't seek great emotions. When people ask me if I'm a man of faith, I reply that God believes in me, he believes that I am still going to do something reasonable with my life. Or actually with the rest of it, I have no idea, how long.

When I made a decision about the 'leap of life', my own shadow tapped its own forehead. When Pirandello enabled Mattia Pascal a second life, he gave him financial assistance. My fortune consists of five books of my authorship, a few photographs, a medal and a set of chess found by Camden Road. I could fit all my possessions in my pockets. And finally my most precious treasure – freedom. Thanks to freedom, after thirty years of fruitless work and marriage, at the age of sixty I finally saw the sea. Thanks to freedom I have arrived six miles away from Cambridge, to the bottom of a former lake, which died three centuries ago due to considerable dehydration. Thanks to freedom whenever I'm being asked about my well-being, I keep saying that for me each and every day is good.

I am a happy man. It's not just a simple conviction, it's a fact. This confidence wasn't shaken by sleeping in the door of the church on the corner of Camden and Hilldrop Road for eighteen months. It was a truly good place. The only place, where I slept when I was homeless. Not to mention some isolated nights spent in the Regent's Park or in Hampstead, right in the back of George Orwell's house.

That second park and its surroundings had a magical influence on me. John Keats, John Constable, George Orwell, Virginia Woolf. Outstanding yet tragic figures. Boudica, Guy Fawkes, Jack Straw, associated with Wat Tyler and his revolt, the owner of the Spaniards Inn, Herbert Spencer and Karl Marx, all resting amicably on a nearby cemetery. And finally, Sigmund Freud. The man who told the Nazi: I am going to die, certainly, I can't avoid it. Not on your terms, however.

Traces of Charles Dickens, George Bernard Shaw can still be found in the neighbourhood. All this appeals to the imagination, narrows the distance to people known from textbooks or their works. I can't stop smiling thinking about Orwell. Although I'm not very keen on his works, some episodes of his biography are extraordinarily close to mine. We have missed each other a lifetime as I was born a year after his death. In London we walked on the same streets, we drunk cider on the same benches. We both knew the poverty very well. He overcame the shame and has become a beggar for some time - I also accepted money from people. The homelessness is noticeable. A backpack, a sleeping bag. Very often people gave me money even though I have never asked for it. I tried to manage on my own way, by checking the phone booths and the parking meters. Eric Arthur Blair probably didn't have such an opportunity.

If homelessness is immoral, my road to Emmaus can only be a road to a moral resurrection. I can't find, however, anything immoral in the in the fact of being homeless. The ancients used to say: all roads lead to Rome. I say: various roads lead to Emmaus. There is a specific symbolism hidden in this sentence, not deliberate, but very true.

I have been dying a few times. Each time I was forced to do it from the beginning, never finishing. It's not a pleasant occupation. I can say with a clear conscience that I fully understand what the English expression 'near-death experience' means. Twice in my childhood I was close to vanishing into nothingness. I was four when I was sitting on a railway track, in front of a steam locomotive. I was sitting just a few yards from the door of the train station, which, at that time, was my home. I was sitting there, playing with stones. The train operator almost went grey when he saw me. He was about to start the train when he remembered something and went down on the platform. He would later walk in the glory of a possessed person, as according to his story, a sky-blue mist had stopped him from starting the locomotive. The prudent train operator is probably already dead, but the story of my careless, childish play has lived in his family ever since. A few years later my family was poisoned with carbon monoxide. The gas filled the whole room, from the ceiling, stopping half a yard above the floor, maybe a yard. We have been trying repeatedly to stand up, just to fall unconsciously on the floor again and again. The secret killers like this sort of fun. Finally mother managed to open the window. On that day we couldn't even count on missing school, but our mother fell ill.

I remember a flash point in my long life. It was when I left the office one day and suddenly I stopped in the middle of the pavement, thunderstruck. I had no place to go. Emptiness. I hanged myself. But the humanists haven't respected my decision. They straightened by force the fingers of the Death, clenched around my neck, and forced their air into my lungs. Saint Peter hasn't slept already and he found my file. He arched his eyebrows with amazement, reading the previous entries. At the time, when down below people kept flashing the sun into my eyes, he sunk his angelic pen in a blue ink:

15

– Once again he didn't show up – he wrote.

He put away my file and closed the gate.

In the meantime the experts kept digging in my body and my brain. The minute I admitted I made a mistake, I realised I lost again. A free man died, a deserter was born. Freud would have understood it:

– You can't live, you can't die, you poor, poor man.

I should have said:

- I need to live if you don't let me do anything else, but not on your terms.

Nevertheless, a restored nature of a deserter has sealed my lips and the repairers of the burnt out light bulbs washed their hands.

A few years later I met the Death once again. It was a frosty evening when I left the restaurant. The Death came up to me when I sat on a bench to smoke a cigarette and I fell asleep. Perhaps she shrugged her shoulders:

- Is that you again?

She grabbed my hands and injured the tips of my fingers by frostbite, the fingertips are still bothering me to the present day. By a strange twist of fate Stan was just passing by. He carried me on his back for about 200 metres. He left me in the stairs to my house. Of course you haven't met Stan. Very few people actually knew him, apart from the regulars of local pubs, the police and prison guards. His life is summarised in police records describing minor brawls and thefts. I, however, remember him fondly. Not because he saved my life. He did it selflessly, instinctively. It could have been justified as afterwards we often drunk together, we drunk a tank of vodka just the two of us. Stan died the way he lived: of heart failure, on the stairs of a restaurant. Irony not missed. Shortly after that the pub itself fell into oblivion.

I reminisce through my writing these closer and more distant deaths without a profound reason. To be honest, I'm not sure, why am I doing it. I would be grateful if somebody considers it a sort of revenge on the literature and read

16

biographies, which lacked sense even more. One good reader – that's the correct measure of a writer's success. I reminisce my deaths in words also because someone might consider them as one of my ways to Emmaus. And that would be my other good reader. There's one more reader that might find this interesting. That's a reader who has experienced love fading away, who understood and forgave the man, but not his handwriting. A reader who won't be capable of understanding, how the same shapely words could express love and yet file petitions. How could they worship and calumniate. That's another of my ways to Emmaus, probably the broadest, well-worn road. A road of a man who was born and who lived in the epoch of hand-written letters.

The Death, or rather its personification, has certainly gave up on me, perhaps I would remind her of myself one day, when I yearn for a rest. Today, however, in April 2013, no one is threatening or blackmailing me with it.

Around thirty years ago in one of the newspapers I saw World Press Photo prize-winning pictures. One of them presented a tramp, sleeping on a street bench. Unshaven, bundled with some rags. The title said: 'Rejected by the society'. Maybe I have already been homeless back then, although I wasn't aware of that. The hypocrisy of that title shocked me, later it made me laugh. Who's rejecting whom? Right now, when I'm writing about how for five hundred days and five hundred nights I have been consciously homeless, I recollected that picture. I recollected the comments written by my compatriots on the Internet forum, describing the homeless as the dregs of society. I could almost see them. They are my employers from London, who would first illegally hire a man with no prospects for a normal job, just to rob him a minute later of his few lousy pounds. Fragrant, replete parvenus. Robbers who reject those who were robbed. I may be bending the situation to my literary needs. I am doing it consciously. The money, which they hadn't intended to pay me, could have covered my one-year rent.

I am a happy man. When I think of those, whom I have already mentioned or would mention soon, it's not because I nurse a grudge against them. I don't feel resentment towards them, I don't think I'm better than them. I'm writing about all this without any major emotions. They are who they are. I don't want to fix them or preach them. They are my past. They are so far away behind me that I keep wondering sometimes if they are actually alive or maybe I made them up.

Various roads lead to Emmaus. Mine was quite straight. I slept in the door of a church, or rather a former church. A few older, ailing people lived there. I didn't care for a contact with them, but it couldn't be completely avoided. We used to share with each other cigarette butts, which we collected on the streets. In the morning I rolled my sleeping bag, hid it in a wooden locker and I moved ahead. There were several places where one could eat breakfast. First I directed my steps towards Tottenham Court Road. In one of the side roads there was a church, where one could get a pound. In the morning many homeless used to gather there, a truly international assembly.

On weekdays I later directed my steps toward the West London Day Centre. Before I became a regular there, I could use the pound to buy some food. Later I began receiving weekly vouchers. Karen, a wise and good woman, didn't give them away in vain. Just a hint of her good will was enough to change one's life. No one who made such a big decision was left without help. This is how, after the decision and a few months of waiting, I became a companion and after three years spent in London, among which half of it I spent on the street, I moved near Cambridge.

If you had spent a year and a half a few metres from a busy street, in a place safe from rain or snow, but not free of cold and wind, on a hard floor, you need to learn living under a roof from the beginning. Two square metres of concrete has been replaced with a furnished room with a bathroom. The all-night car, bus and motorcycle noise has been replaced with a garden silence. Cigarette butts, collected on the streets, have been replaced with original tobacco. At first all these put me to trouble. A bed, silence, tobacco. I came with a considerable reserve of cigarette ends and I didn't get rid of them. I smoke them all, to the last one.

Home. I am learning everything from the beginning and I keep repeating, like a little child:

- Home, this is my home.

I have my ashtray, my coffee mug, a bookshelf, where I keep my music CDs and my movies, a notebook which facilitates my writing. A chessboard on a table on the right with pieces and pawns ready for action. I'm sitting next to the window, in front of which the flowers are growing and the rabbits are looking for their favourite grass, while the robins are perching on a sill. The window isn't too airtight and sometimes the cold forces me to wear a warm sweater or a jacket. How come, when I was living on the street and was looking at homes, I didn't feel the warmth of their interiors? That's probably a topic for Dickens, not for me. Right now, through a cold airstream, I can feel the interference of my old world. I have switched places with someone who lived in this room before me. He went back to the street, because he didn't respect what has been offered to him. I took his place.

This not unprecedented swap reminds me of Junior. He once joined us in Regent's Park. It was a hot day, so we hid the reserve of cider in the shade of a big tree. The squirrels have already quitted bugging us. All the chestnuts that we have collected for them on the way, have been placed in squirrels' larders. One could smell hay and roses. A fierce tobacco smoke from cigarette butts and a scent of warm cider squeezed in that mixture of fragrances. If there actually is a person who could imagine this mixture of scents. As usual, the leisurely bivouac has been accompanied with stories. The homeless, at least those whom I have met, usually had well-prepared stories on their previous lives and the reasons of their current situation. Disbelief in those stories would be a serious blunder, a blind faith would indicate stupidity.

I don't know if Junior told the truth or if he just shared his legend. Living on the street has adjusted my sensitivity at low frequencies. He approached us, because he wanted to get acquainted with us and our life, so that he could comprehend it and reflect it in a movie. This excerpt of a contemporary reality, presented by him from the journalist point of view, was supposed to be a gate to the adult professional life. He wanted to leave his family house for some time to get to know living on the streets and tell about it to the listeners and the viewers.

- It's not the first and probably not the last of such attempts – I thought then.

A young man wants to be in a place, which I have been approaching for years. He wants to go from the beginning of his life to the evening of my life as if he was crossing the street. With each cup of cider our interest with the new acquaintance grew and there were more and more candidates for the leading part.

- The Oscars are scattered around the lawn in Regent's Park – I thought. - They are lying, drinking cider, smoking tobacco from cigarette butts. Soon they would start buying mansions, cars and prying paparazzi would make their lives difficult.

Perhaps it was Lee Hoplin, perhaps Hugh Jackman during the "Live below the line" campaign, perhaps someone else. A descendant of Baden-Powell's scout or maybe one of Jack London's characters. He wanted to fall into the street life like a Prometheus and snatch a fire for his youthful enthusiasm. The venture that he undertook was the cause for hundreds of broken pens of whole generations of writers. The lenses and the cameras of well-known and respected authors have never managed to reflect it. Of course the topic is and will be tempting. The author should, however, know the answers to

20

several questions. What he would like to present, why does he want to do it, what means would he use and who would be the addressee of his work. If it would be the "rejected by the society", it would be a waste of time. It would just be a perfect bullshit.

When Abbé Pierre first appeared on the Radio Luxembourg, I was three years old. I can only imagine, in what circumstances and why the Emmaus was born. Today I am inside of it, I am a part of it. I am saying: this is my home. I have been approaching it through many ways. I arrived empty, like a case made of soft matter. I am now filling up and straightening up. I am arranging all my new belongings, experiences, friendships inside of me. Ecce homo? I do not know.

The time of asking questions is behind me, the thistle will not bloom for me anymore. In spite of that or perhaps for this reason I am a happy man.

One Man's Meat
Phil Arnold

Woke at dawn.
Stretched and looked around.
Perfect morning.
Sunlight through the green.
Sky gaining colour.
Bird-noise to wake the dead.

Early to rise... keeps you out of the lock-up, especially when you're an old bloke like me and your home's a couple of shrubs in the park. Wanted to get up early anyway. Had an idea that couldn't wait. Keeping me awake all night. Had to get it down before it disappeared with the cynicism of the day.

Book was coming on - really developing. But I wasn't getting any younger.

First one up.
Best time of the day.
Best spot in the park.

I had to wait for it though. Waiting list a mile long. Perfect spot you see?

In the sun and out of the wind; northeast aspect; close transport and public amenities; all mod cons; retirement special. Started out on the benches and worked my way up – little by little. Now here I am – top of the heap!

Can't afford to be slack though. Plenty waiting around if you're late. Missing presumed dead. Cut your throat for two bob and leave the change in your pocket.

Washed the wrinkles and stubble in the fountain. Fresh and cold. Good to be alive. Wouldn't be dead for quids. Busting for a leak though. Bladder getting weak. Or maybe the sound of running water.

Usual place.

Vines and tangle (nature's toilet).

Too late!

Walloper on the trail.

Saw me shaping up to the shrub and moved in. Saw him first and started to smell the flowers and examine the foliage. Nature lover from way back. Well, the Sweet Pea always was my favourite flower.

"Morning Officer."

Surly expression.

Usual third degree.

Had the price of a meal.

Made him worse.

No sense of proportion.

No depth of character.

Time was when you could talk to a cop on the beat for hours. Not now though.

No social graces.

Pallid.

Flabby.

Discontented.

Suspicious.

Down in the mouth.

On the take.

Don't understand the code.

Railway dunny again!

Never mind. Needed more paper for the book anyway. First footprints on the dew, bar the copper's. Fast ones at that. Over the road. Into the shadows.

Brrrr!

Chilly.

Concrete.

Hard.

Jars the bones.

Down the ramp.

Breeze at my back.

Early morning sweeper kicking up dust.

"Go easy China. Still be there tomorrow."

Grunted. Swept some more in my direction.

Bad for the chest.

Bastard!

Only one rule, these young blokes. Dog eat dog and I'm too old to argue. Put up or shut up.

I shut up.

Into the land of the waist high mirrors. Two blokes there already. Department store dummies. Looking at the ceiling, then the floor; anything but talk.

Don't understand troughs. Never use 'em m'self. What's mine's my own and I'll choose who does the looking. Worth a couple of bob for the privacy of the cubicle. Wealth of reading matter to boot. Not as good as it used to be though. No subtlety. Artwork's not a patch either.

Relief!

Glorious!

Worth waiting for.

Thought it'd go on forever.

Grabbed some pages for the book, sharpened my pencil on the concrete and left the stench behind.

Up the ramp.

Towards the daylight.

Sweeper having a smoke.

Blank eyes.

Dead fish.

Hurried home to work.

Found a bench in the sun and got to it. The idea was even better on paper. Went down easy. Took off on its own. Wrote itself. Page after page. Couldn't keep up. (Bloody arthritis.) Took a good two hours. Twelve hundred words. A good morning's work.

Read back over it and licked it into shape. Tied up the loose ends. Halfway through the first draft. Put it with the rest and went for a walk to the harbour. Thought I might pick up something for breakfast. Pickings are good if you're early enough.

Walked through the park.

Hands in pockets.

Sun on my back.

Nature's medicine.

Stimulates the system.

Passed a couple of love-sick calves.

Hand in hand.

Gazing at each other.

Love's young dream.

Their systems didn't need stimulating.

Too much bloody stimulation already!

Well and truly hooked.

Black and white.

Full church job.

Down the aisle.

"Wish 'em luck as we wave…"

Wish 'em luck alright!

Up to their necks in debt.

One born.

One on the way.

House payments.

Car payments.

Telly payments.

Fridge, washing machine, carpet and lawn mower payments…

Not for me!

Stories and marriage don't mix.

Had a girl once though.

Up the aisle.

Penguins and bouquets.

The works.

My folks on Wednesdays for cold meat salad, hers on Sundays for midday roast. Brand new car. Steady job. Nine to Five. Mortgaged to here!

No good though. Ate my heart out. Nothing wrong with her, mind you - nothing at all.

A real little bottler.

A genuine humdinger.

Straight out of House and Garden.

Legs right up to her bum.

But there we go.

All things must pass.

Saw a bin. Full to overflowing. Worth a look. Used to feel embarrassed.

Hunger soon cured that - hunger and human wastefulness.

Salad rolls with barely a bite, whole pieces of fruit.

Bloody disgrace! Found enough for breakfast and headed down to the water.

Young mum coming my way - couple of kids in tow.

She ushered 'em away.

Understandable. Old codger like me. Enough to scare the living daylights.

Tried to reassure 'em. Smiled in their direction. Crooked, toothless smile.

They hurried on.

Ah well.

Guess I won't be asked to baby sit.

Reached the water and spread my meal out. Not as good as it looked. Meagre pickings in fact. Needed a good meal from somewhere. Thought about doing some more writing. Mood had gone though. Starting to feel down. Young mum did it. Didn't hold it against her though. Not her fault. She couldn't know.

Wandered along the harbour past Harry's Café. Breathed in the aroma. Mmmm. Pie 'n' peas'd be good. It'd cheer me up no end. Depression and hunger are bad bed fellows! Thought better of it though. Pension day still a way off and I might need the money before then. Besides, I could get a free Chinese feed from Lucky Charlie's.

Charlie was a good bloke provided you didn't make a welter of it. He'd fix me up a feed of fried rice with sweet and sour sauce. Or maybe some curry. The more I thought about it the better I felt. It put some spring in my step. Kept me going all day. Had to stop m'self from going down too early. You've gotta pick the right time at Charlie's. Too early and you put the regulars off; too late and you miss out on the decent tucker.

Lobbed in about 9.30. Down the alley, round the back. Place seemed a bit different. Couldn't quite pick it. Few silvertails round the front. Maybe Charlie had spruced the place up a bit. Come to think of it, it'd been a while.

Through the back door. Into the kitchen. Hive of industry. Couldn't see Charlie straight off. Asked one of the kitchen hands. Shrugged his shoulders and pointed to a bloke coming towards us. Not Charlie. Moving smartly though. Kitchen knife in one hand and bloody big saucepan in the other.

"Charlie no here no more", he said. "I Wung Lo. You piss off bloody quick."

I held up my hands in surrender.

"Charlie give me tucker," I said quickly, gesturing to my mouth and backing away in case he didn't understand.

He understood alright.

"Charlie no fuckin' here", he screamed, waving the knife and pot in unison. "You piss off bloody quick or I bloody chop."

I pissed off bloody quick.

Out the back door.

Down the lane.

Just in time!

Knife whistled past one shoulder.

Saucepan past the other.

Bloody near thing.

Got the feeling I wasn't the first bloke to try and cadge a meal off the new management. Took off down the street and didn't stop for three blocks. Gasping for air, heart pounding fit to bust. The sudden activity, you see. Not used to it. Thought I was having a heart attack for a moment or two. Took me a while to catch my breath and come back down to earth. Not sure what upset me most – the thought of dying or missing out on that feed.

Strewth! The world was going crazy. Couldn't rely on anyone or anything. No bastard understood the code any more. I could feel myself getting really worked up. They had to be taught. Someone had to bloody teach them. Not that I'm vindictive. Live and let live and all that. But someone had to teach 'em a bloody lesson.

Went back to the park.

Young bloke hanging round.

Surly look.

Gave him short shift.

Not in the mood for it.

I was awake half the night, tossing and turning. Trying to work out a plan. I came up with a beauty just before sun-up.

Perfect.

Right down to the last detail.

Had to wait all week for the right opportunity, though.

Saturday night'd be the go.

Restaurant full of toffs.

Kitchen flat out.

I'd show the bastards!

Had a bit to do first though. Managed to get hold of a couple of decent sized hessian bags and some rope. Cut some holes around the tops of the bags and threaded the ropes through. Revenge is good for the soul. Don't let anyone tell you otherwise.

Stimulates the creative juices.
Gets the adrenaline flowing.
Like a kid again.
Could hardly wait.

Made a phone call about eight then headed down to the fish markets. Called 'round the back of the pet shop on the way and rummaged around. Found just what I was looking for. The markets were practically deserted except for a few wild Toms looking for scraps and a bit of the other. Just what the doctor ordered.

Took some fish out of my pocket. Ponged a bit, but it suited my purpose. Before I knew it half the city's stray cats were hanging around. Quick as a wink I had three in one bag and four in the other.

Couple of scratches.
(Nothing to worry about.)
Went like clockwork.
They struggled like mad.
Squealing and squirming.
Biting and scratching.
The more the better.
So far so good.
Now for the fun.

Set off for Wung bloody Lo's through the back streets.
Perfect timing!
Place was packed!
Walked in through the front door, straight up to the girl at the counter. She looked a bit startled.

"It's okay love," I said, loudly as I could. "Tell the boss it's the Catman."

Cats were going berserk.
All I could do to hold them.

People craning their necks.

Girl getting flustered.

Didn't know which way to turn.

"You wait outside please?"

"No need to worry, love," I said, giving her a nod and a wink. "I can see the boss is busy. I'll just take 'em in m'self".

I strode through the restaurant, holding the bags up high. The cats screamed and struggled for all they were worth and the little girl hurrying after me.

"Don't worry folks.

Tucker's on the way.

Won't be long."

By this time the boss and half the kitchen staff had arrived, yabbering and flapping their arms and wondering what was going on.

"There you are boss," I said. "Sorry I'm late. Couldn't get here sooner. I'd have come round the back but I wasn't game after last time, eh. They're alive I'm afraid, but at least you know they're fresh."

With that I walked into the kitchen and emptied the contents of both bags on the floor.

Pandemonium!

Cats everywhere.

Skin and fur flying.

Cook chasing 'em with his meat cleaver.

Food all over.

Sauce up-ended.

Bloody mess!

A few cats got into the restaurant. They tore across the tables and up the curtains.

Patrons jumping.

Women screaming

Wung Lo chasing.

Absolute bloody chaos!

Emptied a bag of rat's poo behind the fridge (courtesy of City Pets) and slipped a carcass in the freezer while everyone was preoccupied. Stayed as long as I dared then joined the rush to the exit.

Beat most of the patrons out, but only just. Passed the health inspector coming in. Someone must've given him the tip. Funny that. Reckon the place was empty in less than two. Took off as fast as I could, ducking and dodging my way up the street. Ran out of puff pretty quick though. Not as young as I used to be. Headed for a laneway and stopped to get my breath back. Ticker racing ninety to the dozen.

Half stood,
Half sat.
Against a wall
Gasping and laughing.
Tears streaming.
Reliving the whole bloody thing.
The look on Wung Lo's face said it all.
Couldn't have gone better.
Strictly to plan.
Spot on.
Funniest thing you ever saw.
What a lark.
That'd teach 'em.

Half tempted to sneak back for another look. Too risky though.

Just decided to clear out when I saw them: Wung Lo's mates coming towards me, bloody big sticks in hand.

Bugger!

Should've kept going. Thought of running but too late. Reinforcements at the other end.

Ambushed.
No way out.
Smiling faces.
Slapping the sticks into their hands.
No point running.
No point fighting.
Just make it worse.

"Go on you bastards, do your worst."
No sense of humour.
No sense of proportion.
Just don't understand the code.

Phil Arnold

Phil Arnold is a teacher, musician, composer, playwright and fiction writer living in Sydney, Australia. Though he spends most of his professional time directing community and school band programmes, he is also a freelance writer/editor, having published articles in professional magazines, and has written several musical plays, all of which have been performed several times.

Phil has written fiction since childhood and recently completed a Masters degree in Creative Writing through the University of Sydney where he studied under award-winning novelist Sue Woolfe.

He is currently working towards the completion of his first novel.

The New Home
Hugh Kellett

January 2000, Edinburgh

As she put down the tea cup, the porcelain cup with its pink pattern of interwoven roses, she wondered why it kept shaking on the saucer. It seemed to have taken on a mind of its own, waves rippling out from the centre sending small globlets of tea over the edge into the saucer; and the more she tried to stop it the stronger the movement seemed to become. Flustered, she returned it to the tray on the carved mahogany side table and decided, not for the first time, to fill it slightly less full in future. She inspected the cup and watched for more movement in the tea as it sat there on the table, but the waves had subsided. The traffic outside did rattle the windows a little so maybe that was it. Or maybe it was just the new apartment she was getting used to. She parted the nets to look out on to the Merchiston Road, some fifty feet or so away: the traffic was light. It was 4.30 in the morning. The nets gave off that smell of dust that always seemed to cling to them. That was the first thing she had to change.

She looked down at her wrists. Even she was taken aback by how thin they appeared and how loosely the gold bracelet seemed to hang. How blue-white and veiny, translucent almost, they were, so much so she fancied she could almost see the bones. She held out and extended her fingers, trying her best to unwind them a little as she did each morning. It was true, they did seem to shake a little more each day.

Her new apartment was in a good part of Edinburgh. Built at the end of the Victorian age, there were forty separate flats in the block, mainly two-bedroomed, but spacious with large sitting rooms. The lifts had concertinaed steel gates that still ran smoothly on their bearings and, though heavy, were quite easy to operate once you got the knack. They were original too, in good condition considering their age, with a faint smell of heavy lubricating oil and a muffled winding mechanism that whirred away somewhere in the basement when you pressed the button, followed several seconds later by the lift actually moving. Inside it was all wood-lined, like an old railway carriage, with a single light screwed into a socket in the ceiling. The rear wall held a mirror, though the lighting ensured this did not always deliver a flattering reflection. The lift's brass handles, smooth and shiny, were, according to the particulars and stressed by the agent, buffed twice weekly by the cleaners. Apart from the floor buttons there was a further button marked "In Case of Emergency", but it wasn't clear who would answer this were such an event to present itself.

The lifts served the four floors of the building, each level having ten flats. Outwardly the flats were uniformly anonymous, bearing only a number, and sporting in some cases a doormat on the outside, but inside they were generally genteel, perhaps quite grand even, with small fireplaces converted to gas, large bay windows and a sizeable hall from which the other rooms were accessed. Those energetic enough to use the stairs would find themselves in a marble-style stairwell with a brass hand rail and with tall, greenish, frosted glass windows at each landing that ensured privacy from the adjacent blocks, from the outside world at large. Although she had lived there scarcely more than a week, she had only heard rather than seen any of her neighbours, and this as but a distant murmur, as the walls were thick. From inside the apartment she could just hear the lift gates opening and shutting. The only other sound was the occasional rattle of the letter box as the postman delivered and, apart from a distant roll of traffic, the sound of the one o'clock gun from the castle, which she usually anticipated rather than necessarily heard and which signalled her time for lunch and radio news.

She had not really planned on taking the apartment, but, with her solicitor, finally reasoned it was for the best - central, solid, secure - far more suitable than her previous home in the Old Town with its steep stairs and creaking floors, and she had been moved in with little fuss. Many of her boxes lay stacked and unpacked in the spare bedroom, but she had filled her new bedroom cupboard with her own things and set up a variety of her favourite vases, in strategic places around the flat, filling them with artificial flowers, sweet peas and roses. To the mantelpieces she added an assortment of framed photographs, places cherished in the past - Paris particularly, and a beach scene somewhere - noticing with a touch of frustration that one of them, of a young man in the military uniform of a British army lieutenant, with a recognisable 40s smile and hairstyle, had a crack in the glass. Had this happened in the move she wondered, or sometime previously at the old house? It seemed so difficult to remember some of these things.

One o'clock and she went in search of the portable radio in the bedroom. Mistakenly, she opened the wrong door and found herself in a broom cupboard. It was no matter, she would find her bearings. She turned on the little transistor, and returned to the sitting room, having first made herself a little treat of biscuits and camembert in the kitchen. The news was about something called the Millennium bug and she wondered quizzically what manner of creature this might be, and whether it could come to Scotland. At the same time she heard the letter box clank and two letters dropped on to the carpet, the one in a brown official looking envelope, the other in blue, with what looked like a foreign stamp. She needed her glasses. She reached into her pocket for them, only to find, to her slight surprise and no small shame, that she was still in her nightgown.

She set her little feast on the table, donned her glasses and opened the first letter, the brown one. It was from the driving people and was written in somewhat opaque language but seemed to be saying that, as she had now reached 75, she would have to undergo some sort of medical and that her licence would no longer be valid should she fail to comply with this request. Driving had always been one of her great dreams, travelling generally in fact, but she had not driven for some years as the traffic had got so bad, and since she had nearly collided on several occasions with cyclists and pedestrians who had appeared from nowhere. She had sold the car, so who needed a licence anyway? She put down the circular and, taking two hands to the knife, cut into the rind of the camembert that oozed pleasingly. She liked this sort of soft food these days as it was easier on her teeth. And camembert had its own evocative power too, rich and redolent of Paris, of baguettes, bottles of cidre bouche, and champagne…

She mused.

She turned the other envelope on its back, wiped the knife and steered it painstakingly into the little crack slitting it open quite neatly, albeit with a jerky bird-like movement. It was quite a long letter. Good she thought, and started to read.

My Dear Mother, it began, and she smiled.

I hope you are well and that your move will go (has gone?) smoothly. Where to begin? I have been travelling now for three weeks and have reached Menorca. It's cold but bright as I write but I wanted to visit out of season and the hotel in Mahon is less than half the price at this time of year and thankfully nearly empty. But I am getting ahead of myself, let me go back to leaving Scotland. I took the train south for Kings Cross, you know they still call it somewhat romantically The Flying Scotsman, but it lived up to its name and all connections from there to Dover were surprisingly easy and actually ON TIME!

She noticed the letter was quivering slightly but uncontrollably in her hand. The Flying Scotsman! Her glance shifted to the photograph with its broken glass on the mantelpiece. That had been their first real time together, 1943, just after they had become engaged, after all the letters between them from the French front. Her fiancé! He had

40

come back on leave and she had met him in London where he had proposed, giving her the gold bracelet she still wore. He had hired a room in a hotel and had pressed her for intimacy, but she had demurred, half against her will, until they were "properly married". The next evening, on The Flying Scotsman northbound to meet her parents they had dined on steak and kidney pie, as she now quite clearly remembered, he talking of France, teasing her about the French girls, and promising to take her to Paris when it was all over. For her part, later in evening, she had again wriggled from his warm embrace outside his sleeper berth.

The letter continued: *The crossing was eventfully rough with people being sick everywhere, but it all subsided when we reached the other side and I was soon on board the Paris train, quite snug in fact in a compartment. The Gare de Nord was its normal frantic self and I got out of there as fast as possible although the taxi queue was endless as usual. I settled on a small hotel near the Jardins de Luxembourg, where we used to stay remember, although that particular hotel is no more...mort!*

The Gare du Nord! The Jardins de Luxembourg! Again, the names struck home with a kind of ferocious nostalgic clarity, names and places that had lain buried these many years.

Well I did pretty much what you do in Paris, strolled and ate shellfish and sat outside the cafes under the welcome glow of the new gas heaters they use in winter. Waiters still dressed properly in tie and apron, charming and attentive if you remember to say Bonjour (as the British invariably don't) and predictably surly if you don't. When will we learn... maybe there should be a sign (in English of course!?)

Anyhow I poked about the Seine banks and visited Pere Lachaise cemetery the afternoon before leaving. What a place to reside for eternity, amongst the greats! I also visited Baudelaire's grave (or graves should I say) in Montparnasse. Did you know he was originally buried in the family plot at

41

the corner of the cemetery, but, on opening the Will, his executors discovered express instructions that he be buried as far as possible from his parents? So they thought for a bit and moved him as far as they could, using good Gallic reasoning and expediency, to a plot diagonally opposite. Bizarrely, they never changed the inscription on the original tomb, so he is in fact in two places.

She paused, a little confused, to reflect on this point and reached for another piece of cheese. Then she read on:

I had made up my mind to continue south by train. The countryside is so beautiful and develops so marvellously as you go further south. And your fellow French travellers are so civilised, calling you Monsieur, and wishing Bon Appetit! to perfect strangers! It wasn't all plain sailing as the train got held up at the border and arrived in Barcelona late and I had to scramble across the city by taxi to the ferry - but just made it - and I was bound for Mahon. It really is so much more exciting arriving at an island by sea and we got to Menorca at 7 in the morning.

Menorca. She had been there in 1938, aged 13, when it was still mainly undiscovered, with very little in the way of tarmac. The island was crisscrossed by a network of pot-holed cart tracks that ran hither and thither, narrowly contained within the confines of exquisitely constructed dry-stone walls. You could walk for miles along these tracks and see no-one but the occasional peasant farmer in the field tilling melons, or a donkey bearing an impossibly heavy load, swinging between the walls, towing a water bowser.

Occasionally, in the rockier areas covered with scrubby grasses and wild thyme you might come across a shooter, clutching a pair of thrushes. At the end of one such path, not too far from where the family was staying, she had found a small hunting lodge perched on a rocky cliff by the water's edge. It was little more than a bothy really, built like an igloo, whitewashed and isolated against the impossible blue of the sea. She had assumed it was empty but was planning on avoiding it as who knew what might be inside. As it happened she was too late and a man had appeared. An old man, about 60, maybe more, fat and handsome at the same time, with blue eyes and olive skin that was perhaps not his natural colour. He wore only a pair of faded khaki shorts and old sandals. She had thought again about making her escape but had dithered. What would they say, she a 13 year old girl and he a near-naked man? But he called her in English and, leaving the bothy, walked slowly to the sea, some distance from her. He lit a cigarette and he beckoned her to follow. They sat on a rock together where she listened to his story, a tale that she could recall almost word for word 62 years later, as the past surged up.

He was Dutch. He had come on honeymoon. He had been married to the most beautiful girl. She had gone water-skiing in the bay, this bay. She had fallen and disappeared below. As the motor boat came back to find her she had resurfaced unexpectedly and the propeller had sliced her head open. That was it, she was gone, buried in the cemetery of Sant Lluis nearby. And he, he had sat on the rock each day for a fortnight after the event, willing her to return, unable to leave. Until the owner of the land had come to him and offered him the shelter of the bothy while he recovered. Except he never did. He bought the bothy and stayed. That was 40 years ago next summer he had said, handing her a sprig of thyme. She had asked if there had been anyone else, and in his thick Dutch accent he had shaken his head: She was irreplaceable.

She heard the words again clearly, as if it were yesterday.

The letter drifted on and signed itself Ben, but now she was only half attending, her reverie only being interrupted by the unfamiliar sound of the doorbell. She tucked the letter neatly back into its envelope and went to answer, calling through the door for identification. It turned out to be the solicitor, whom she had forgotten had promised to visit that afternoon. Wiping her eyes and remembering herself, flustered a little, she quickly threw on a housecoat. The lawyer entered and was ushered into the sitting room, making appropriate small talk about how nice the new flat looked. She nodded in agreement as she bumbled into the kitchen to make tea.

He met her on her return, alerted by the rattling tray and took it off her. They drank and smiled and discussed whatever it was he'd come about.

As he got up to leave he noticed the envelope on the table. Not realising it had been opened, he picked it up and read the writing on the front.

"This is addressed to the previous person who lived here," he said, "I'll see it's forwarded for you. All part of the service."

When he'd gone, she sat down again and looked at the photograph on the mantelpiece. They never had been married because he had never returned. They had never got to Paris.

She had never sought another.

He was irreplaceable.

But here in her new home, she had known for the first time what it might have been to be a mother.

Hugh Kellett

Hugh Kellett won the poetry prize at school and was delighted before learning he was the only entrant, but it set him on the road. He then studied languages at Oxford, where his plays and musicals were performed, and has been playing around with words in London advertising agencies most of his life. Despite this, or perhaps because of it, his short story themes tend towards the nostalgic and rueful, and probe human yearnings for self-fulfilment with their associated secret feelings of regret and failure.

Hugh also writes comedy, and his book *Glitzch!* which dramatises the havoc that can be wrought by predictive text is due out late autumn 2013.

Number One Girl
Jane Carmichael

It's only 5am but already it's almost light. I'm sitting in the little room again, the one with the green curtains. The heavy material has lost its grassy gleam, fading around the edges like an old newspaper. They have not been pulled completely across and I can see the feathery leaves of the beech tree outside the window. The trickling soft summer light makes me feel as though I am floating in a fish tank, fronds of weed swaying against the glass.

I like it here, in this chair, cosy in the warmth of what promises to be another beautiful day. Summer has come early this year, my sweet peas are already trying to bud and my runner beans have swarmed their way up the bamboo canes. This room soothes me, in a way that my own bed does not. I woke abruptly again this morning, a cold sweat filmed across my chest, like dew on a spider's web.

I was dreaming of you, of course.

This room, this chair, more or less unchanged in over two decades. I'm always meaning to get round to updating it, but somehow up here on the third floor, it's tucked away and forgotten, like the tower where Rapunzel slept for a hundred years.

I like to sit here and remember when you were just a tiny thing. When you were four months old, you had just started sleeping through the night. Some days you would make it all the way through to 7am – when the world was already up and bustling about, but other days I'd hear your croaking nightclub singer wail begin at 4.30 or 6, or most usually at 5, that in-between time, right now, that's not night or day, a pearly, magical netherworld.

I'd come into the room and lift you, sleep-soaked from your cot, damp ringlets clinging to your forehead. Gently settling myself in this chair, balancing you on a cushion on my lap, your arms and legs would jerk with excitement as you rooted furtively for my milk. Often, my top would already be drenched before you managed to latch on, two wet patches like crying eyes weeping their way through the cotton fabric. I can almost feel the ache and pull, the soothing relief of being emptied, as I sit here now. But I can't let go yet, can't feel any relief, not until you're safe in my arms.

I know sometimes I love you too much and too hard. You were always meant to have brothers and sisters to share the burden. We wanted to have a big family – your dad was one of four, I was one of three, but I lost so many babies and the trying started to wear away at us until we were barely held together, like a threadbare heel. I couldn't do it any more, so we stopped with you, our Number One Girl. I hope I haven't driven you away.

I can't help thinking about you. What is it like, where you are? Your emails and phone calls don't tell me much. I know you're not allowed to say more than you do. Sometimes we talk about TV programmes – I've started watching Eastenders again just so that we can talk about the plot-line, what's happening to Dot, who the father of Stacey's baby is. It seems funny that you are there, in the middle of a desert, switching on the same programmes as me, seeing the same characters. I think it helps you forget the drama of the life that you are really living. I'm sure you've seen things that no young girl should have to bear.

It is strange how we always end up talking about the soaps, or the weather, like polite strangers at a garden party. I tell you about my plants, and you humour me by listening, and hmming in the right places. It's perfect summer weather at the moment, most of the days are fresh and warm, though by the end of the long days, thunderbugs squirm like tiny specks of ash on my arms and the summer rain falls heavily at night, making everything glittering damp and verdant.

In turn, you tell me what you can about the place where you are. You sleep in a tent with three other girls, hanging fluffy pink lights around the mirror and reading gossip magazines, when you are not working 14 hour days. You eat in a canteen and take freezing cold showers. I can't imagine the kind of heat you are feeling, so hot you can lose half a stone in a day, under that heavy gear of yours. And you tell me that it's gritty. You've described the dust, the way it gets everywhere – in your ears and eyelashes and teeth. I have no frame of reference for what you are going through – finding sand in my butties at the beach can't really compare.

'Summer Fun' they called your tour. I heard your OC joking with one of the others as you left. "Let's go build some sand castles, boys and girls," he said. I didn't hear any more after that. I couldn't look as you got on the bus, couldn't wave at my brave girl, because I knew that if I did, I'd run after you and wail and sob and tear my hair and say "No, don't go, there's been a terrible mistake, you must bring my baby back."

I have been counting the days until you come home, marking them off on the calendar like a child waiting for Christmas. Sometimes I don't hear from you for weeks at a time. That is the hardest part, when my letters and parcels feel like they are being sent into a void. The worst part is that I know that when there is a blackout it's because someone out there has been hurt, or worse. None of you are allowed to make any contact with the outside world, until next of kin have been notified. Someone, somewhere is finding out that their loved one is never coming back.

We are so close now, though, you've nearly made it through. "Part of the job, Mum," you tell me. "Good for my career prospects," but I never understood why you have to do what you do in the Army. Why couldn't you have just been a doctor or nurse in a hospital? There was no need to thrust yourself out there, put yourself square in the middle of things. Don't get me wrong, of course I am proud, so proud. The things you have done, the places you have been, and you've only been in a couple of years. You're fighting for your country, even if the rest of your country doesn't quite understand why.

You tell me "Watch the news, Mum, see the good we're doing, see how we're helping," but I haven't been able to watch the news for months. I can't bear it when they show the planes coming home, the coffins draped with flags, the talk of IEDs and car bombs and suicide missions. I can't hear it, can't listen. I don't want to see other mothers weeping in the streets. And I can't stand the way they count, each week the number creeping up like some sort of sick lottery total. So instead I count down. I started with over 150 days, and now, well now, I hardly dare to look at the calendar, I have to glance at it sidelong, as though if I look at it straight I will jinx things.

Only days to go, 'til I see my baby girl again. I'm so excited about coming to meet you. I've already planned my outfit, and plugged the route to the RAF base into my satnav. The flights never come when they say they are going to, routes are always being changed. I'll undoubtedly be early, so I've got a new book to take, to get through the hours, though I doubt I'll be able to read it, I'll just be gazing at those sliding doors, willing you to walk through with your great big pack full of kit.

I imagine you getting into one of those big aeroplanes, the sort that are hollow inside. You perch on a narrow bench, one of your million and one kit bags by your feet. You are wearing a helmet and uniform, a red and white tag on your arm over the top of your desert combats. You can see out of the open door as the plane lifts off – the grey blocks of the place you have called home for the last six months shrink below you until they look like Lego pieces stuck together in a higgledy-piggledy mess. You'll fly in that plane, then change to another, probably spending an uncomfortable night in an airport somewhere. The next flight you get will be more like a normal one, with tiny tables folded in front of you like bats' wings. Maybe you'll watch a movie, maybe you'll rest, your eyelids drooping as you drift off to sleep.

I think I must have dropped off myself. I can't believe it's nearly eight o'clock. I am late for work. I rush down the stairs, grabbing my towel and dashing towards the bathroom. I rest my specs on the side of the bath and go to climb into the tub. Then I hear it, the doorbell, shrill and insistent. I grab my dressing gown back up and gallop down from the landing, and as I turn the corner into the hall, I look at the calendar full on. The fat Xs look like crosses. A field of unmarked graves.

The doorbell screams again.

My heart shrinks and contracts as I peer through the frosted window. Without my glasses, all I can make out is the khaki green of Army uniforms, the bright sunshine creating two stark silhouettes. I feel sick, and I fumble with the chain. I draw my dressing gown around me, hugging myself tightly, and slowly open the door.

A tall man I don't recognise is standing there, his hands clasped uncomfortably around his beret, wringing it in front of him. I look up at him, trying to read his face. It can't be, I can't believe it can be… I don't want to know. My eyes are already filled with tears, and as he clears his throat, I start to speak too, to stop him, to cut across what I know he is going to say, when a tiny dark haired girl leaps out from behind him. "Surprise!" she shouts. "I'm back Mum, I'm home! Our end of tour date was brought forward! Summer fun officially starts now." And my baby steps inside and wraps her arms around me, hugging me tight, right there on the doorstep. My Number One Girl is home.

Jane Carmichael

Jane Carmichael is a media officer for a UK charity, army wife and mum of two mischievous girls. She says she loves her work "as it basically involves getting the gossip first and deciding who else to let in on the secret!"

Writing has always been an interest and she hopes that eventually 'the book in her' will make it onto the page. That is, once she finishes playing badminton, being walked by the crazy Jack Russell, moving house every five minutes, wiping noses, bouncing on trampolines, reading stories and dancing at Zumba.

Portrait of a Farmer, with Leaves
Jackie Hawkins

I saw it by chance. I was flipping through the TV channels one evening, waiting for my dinner to cook, and I saw his face appear on the screen. I felt a flash of shock and anger so strong that I dropped the remote.

The back fell off and the batteries came out. I watched them roll across the floor, but I couldn't help hearing the presenter's voice.

"…a national figure. This exhibition will bring him back to the prominence he deserves."

"And put up the prices on his work," I said. My voice sounded bitter, even to myself.

My eyes slid to the photo of Katy on the shelf by the window. She smiled at me, the oak trees of Hayes Wood making a halo around her head. Memories tumbled out of me as if from a split sack.

I never go back. It's not home anymore. My parents are dead, the farm sold, my brother Andrew has moved to Scotland. Even Katy isn't there. I couldn't afford to bury her in the village churchyard. I blamed him for that, too.

I hadn't realised how little I'd forgiven him. And it wasn't even his fault.

I stood up and turned the TV off. I needed some air.

John Harper came to Hayes Oak Farm in 1969. I was only nine, and more interested in the Apollo moon landing, but I remember that he arrived at harvest time. He stood at the top of the lane and laughed, but I couldn't hear him for the noise of the combine. He bent down and shouted in my ear.

"They told me it would be quiet and peaceful up here!"

"Who did?"

"The vicar. Is your father around?"

I climbed onto the gate and waved at the harvester halfway across the field. Eventually Dad noticed, and after a few moments the noise was cut off.

It would take Dad a while to walk back across the field, and Mum was in the village with my big brother Andrew. The silence was awkward and I felt I ought to say something. His car was a new, shiny Morris Traveller, one of those estate cars with a wooden frame like an old house, piled high with luggage.

"What's in the boxes?" I asked.

"My life," he said. I stared at him. He smiled. "Clothes and books and toothbrushes. I'm looking for somewhere to rent. I'm a painter."

I understood now. "The cottage?" I said.

John nodded.

"But it doesn't need painting," I said.

He laughed, shook his head, and looked up to greet my father.

He was, of course an artist. Quite a famous artist, it turned out, though not so famous that people like us had heard of him. I looked him up in the library. He'd painted lots of abstract pictures, and lots of pictures of bombed buildings in the Second World War, but the book didn't give any clues as to what he was doing now.

A couple of weeks after he moved in I saw his car parked outside the church, and there he was, perched on a little folding chair, drawing. I wasn't quite brave enough to go into the churchyard and watch him, but over the next few days I found excuses to cycle past the church every day.

Eventually, as I'd hoped, I passed just as he was coming out through the lychgate. I juddered to a halt, supplementing the brakes with my feet.

"Hello, Mr. Harper."

"Hello, Mark." He smiled. I was looking at the sketchbook tucked under his arm.

"Would you like to see what I've been doing?"

"Um. Yes?" I said. I wasn't sure if it was polite to ask or not.

He sat down on the bench under the gate, leaving room for me. He flicked through the sketchbook. All the drawings were of our church. Some were really careful and detailed, others were messy and quick. Some were just of one thing - a window, or a gargoyle, or a single headstone in the graveyard.

"Why churches?" I said.

He shrugged. "After the war I painted quite a lot of bombed churches. It made me interested in them as buildings. I love all the details, like that gargoyle."

"Do you draw anything else?"

"Oh yes, sometimes. I like drawing people working, I might draw your Dad on his tractor one day. But I always come back to churches. I'd like to design a new church, actually, or part of one. The windows, maybe."

"You could do a window for an old church. It wouldn't have to be a new one."

"That's true." He smiled. "Maybe I'll do one for this church, some day."

"Aren't you staying?"

"I like your cottage very much, but I'll run out of local churches eventually."

I liked Mr. Harper much more than the previous tenants, and I wanted him to go on living in the cottage.

"I like those ones best," I said, turning back the pages until I found one of the tidy drawings.

"Do you like art?" he said.

"No," I admitted.

He laughed .

The winter came, and turned, and Mr. Harper stayed on. My parents took to calling him John, and he used their first names too. My brother Andrew discovered that he liked to play chess, and I discovered that he liked conker collecting and bird watching and would learn the names of my favourite cows. It was a bit like having a spare Grandad right next door.

Another year passed. When the next spring came Mr. Harper asked my father if he could convert the old stable into a studio. We watched as the big windows were put in and the roof repaired. He began to paint larger canvases and an etching press came, delivered in a van. It took three men to carry it into the stable. He invited us in to see it and shared a bottle of champagne with us. It was, he said, his seventieth birthday.

I liked cranking the handle for him and watching the cogs turn inside it as the plate passed under the roller. I liked the fact that he trusted me to touch it, but not Andrew. I was more practical, he said. The prints themselves looked wispy and confused to me, but Mr. Harper's agent loved them.

The next November, a few months after the printing press had been set up, Mr. Harper became ill. My mother called the doctor to him, and spent several weeks taking him meals and keeping an eye on him. His agent was up every week with chocolates and letters. He promised, grudgingly that he'd stay indoors in bad weather. No graveyards, no hills. He'd draw the insides of churches, instead.

It fascinated me the way that he would see things I'd never noticed. At church on Sunday I'd spend half the time trying to spot some detail he'd captured. My mother would poke me, and the vicar would frown.

One day after Christmas I was sitting on the kitchen table in Mr. Harper's cottage and eating one of his agent's chocolates when I noticed a new sketchbook on one of the chairs. I picked it up to have a look, I knew he wouldn't mind.

He'd done an ink drawing of the front of a church on the cover.

Mr. Harper came back in.

"Where's this?" I said.

"St Mary's, Barton."

"Oh, yes." I turned the pages. "Oh, look, we've got one a bit like that in our church."

Mr. Harper came to look over my shoulder, and I pointed at his drawing of a carved face. "Hang on a minute," he said.

He fetched one of his other sketchbooks and put it down on the kitchen table side by side for me to compare.

At the top of one of the pillars in the village church was a strange, stone face. It was near the pulpit, and I'd been staring at it, instead of at the vicar, for most of my life. The face was clearly a man's, with bulbous eyes, thick lips, and coarse curly hair. Most remarkably he had two huge wavy leaves coming out of his mouth, one to each side of his face. We'd joked about that in Sunday School, though it never seemed like something you really ought to joke about to me. The stone man was strong, and he looked just as strong in John Harper's drawing.

I looked again at the other sketch, the one from Barton. The man here was at the bottom of something rather than the top. It wasn't carved so well, the face was barely human, with a lipless grimace and eyes like balls under huge brows. The leaves coming from his mouth were cruder, too, strangely lumpy, but were more identifiable. Oak leaves, I was pretty sure. It looked... strong, too, and as if it was laughing, but unkindly.

"They're called Green Men," said Mr. Harper. "Look, here's another. I drew him years ago."

He found a folder in the dresser and passed me a piece of thick paper, torn probably from another sketchbook. There was a simple ink drawing on it. The face was round and bland like the moon. There were two oak leaves coming out of each side of his mouth, the larger ones going up to the side of his face and the smaller ones curling beside his beard.

"That's weird," I said. I looked from one to another again. "They don't look like church things."

"They don't," agreed Mr. Harper. "Nobody knows what they mean, but they might be pagan fertility symbols. Life and harvest and rebirth. Anyway, I've decided to collect them now. Draw as many as possible. Then maybe… a print series, or something more decorative. I don't know."

"Are they old?" I said, still staring.

"Very old," he said. He moved his finger from one drawing to the next. "All of these are fourteenth and fifteenth century."

"How old is that?" I said

"Five hundred years."

I left school in 1978, with two rather poor A levels. I worked with Dad on the farm, I had a girlfriend, and I helped John Harper.

Harper's 'Green Man' series was enormously popular. He worked them up as etchings, each one surrounded by other details of their church's architecture. He was still finding new carvings, writing to parishes and collecting old books of church architecture. Since he was having trouble driving these days, and I'd passed my test, I would take him to visit them.

I enjoyed it. We'd stop for meals in much nicer places than my parents would ever dream of going to, and I saw bits of the country I'd never been to before. We found Green Men in stone, wood and lead, on the outside and inside of churches, on oak panelling and roof bosses and pew ends. Sometimes we stayed the night in small hotels or pubs, and I would drink beer and talk to the bar staff while John drank one whisky and then fell asleep in his chair.

By 1980 we'd pretty much run out of Green Men to collect, and I was working on the farm full-time as my father was beginning to have trouble with his heart. John sketched around the farm, or chatted to my father, or pottered in his studio. He wasn't doing any painting or printmaking any more, but he was working with other craftsmen, designing plates and, as I'd once suggested, stained glass.

On his eightieth birthday we organized a surprise party for him. We invited his agent and his London friends, his nieces and nephews and his friends from the village. His agent paid for caterers (my idea – Mum was too old to do that much cooking) and Andrew painted a giant, though rather wonky, Green Man on the barn door for people to see when they arrived. John loved that.

After we'd all had a few glasses of wine and drunk toasts to John and the farm and anything else anyone could think of, John got out his sketchbook and started to draw us. I'd never seen him draw portraits before. He drew anybody who would keep still for more than five minutes, and my mother dozing in the sunshine.

"Can I draw you, Mark?" he said.

"Of course." I smiled at him and leaned back against the barn door. My shoulder was up against the leafy halo of Andrew's painting.

It was surprisingly difficult to keep still. I desperately wanted to pick something out of my teeth.

"Stop twitching."

Why had I decided to stand with all my weight on one bony shoulder blade? And the sun was in my eyes.

"Are you finished yet?"

"Nearly… Okay, that'll do."

I pushed myself away from the wood and went to peer at his drawing. Andrew joined me and also the daughter of one of John's old friends.

"Wow," she said.

It was both me and not me. My face, yes, but my hair was a mane of oak leaves and a single oak leaf formed my tongue. I

61

looked strong, and ancient. John had drawn me as the Green Man.

"That's amazing," I said.

"It has come out rather well, hasn't it," said John, thoughtfully. "I think I might do something with that."

The girl looked at the picture again, and then at me. "You should grow your hair longer, it suits you," she said. She smiled. "My name's Katy, by the way."

I smiled back. "I'm Mark."

I took over the Hayes Oak Farm in 1982, after my father died of a heart attack, though I did not officially inherit it until my mother died in 1984. Andrew had gone to uni to study English and had no interest in farming. John Harper was still renting the cottage and I remember that we had to reroof it that year. I worked hard, trying to live up to Dad's standards, trying not to miss him too much. I was determined to modernize the farm, bring it up to date, and John encouraged me. Katy drove down from London whenever she could to help me with the accounts or negotiate discounts on equipment. You would not have thought a woman could deal with farm machinery suppliers, but she could drive a harder bargain than I could. The farm thrived.

We married in 1985, in St Matthew's Church. Andrew was my best man. I missed my parents very badly that day, but Katy looked gorgeous and the sun shone.

John nearly didn't come to the marriage service. I hadn't realised how frail he was getting. Katy organized a driver for him and persuaded him to use a wheelchair to get from the car to the church.

He was upset because he hadn't managed to get to the shops to buy us a present. Katy and I weren't bothered, we already had everything we needed. But his agent – by now an old friend of ours, too – suggested that he give us a picture. John brightened up and said he'd give us an etching. Katy smiled.

"I know what I'd really, really like. Could you possibly dig out that drawing you did of Mark at your birthday party? We'd love that."

John looked confused.

"The one of him as the Green Man," she prompted.

"Oh yes, yes, that's a good idea," he said, "The Green Man."

But he still looked confused. I wasn't sure that he remembered the picture at all.

It was Katy that found him. One of the dogs kept barking and barking at the cottage door. After ten minutes or so she realised that there might be something wrong. She couldn't get in through the front door and had to go round the back.

John was lying on the floor in the front room, his body up against the door. For a moment she thought that he was dead, but he was still breathing. She spent thirty minutes waiting for the ambulance, terrified that he would die. No mobiles then, of course; I was still ploughing the top field, my mind on the radio.

At the hospital there was another long wait. They told her that he had fractured his skull and broken his hip and ankle and would have to stay in for a while. She waited until he'd been admitted to a ward, kissed his forehead and came home. We spent that night planning how we could adapt his cottage to make it easier for him to cope, or whether we should even have him live in the farmhouse with us.

After three weeks in hospital John was moved into a nursing home. We visited him regularly, but being away from his studio and all the things he knew seemed to, well, finish him off. Each time we visited he seemed a little more lost. Our conversations did not meet in the middle, and eventually he would stop in mid-sentence and fall asleep. His bones were not healing properly and he was still confined to a wheelchair.

One day we arrived at the nursing home and the receptionist told us that we could only stay a few minutes. He had another visitor, a relative. I was angry; it was a long drive for us.

"Mark, hush." We were walking along the corridor.

"What?"

Katy shrugged unhappily. "She did one of those sad voices. I'm guessing he's… very ill. Maybe they've called his next of kin."

Next of kin? I felt as though we should be his next of kin. It was our family that had been looking out for him all these years. We would still look after him, if we could only get him home.

John was in bed, propped up on pillows but with his eyes closed. His skin was shrivelled against his bones and he was breathing heavily. A man in a suit stood on the far side of the bed, by the window. He turned to look at us, but did not speak. He looked slightly familiar.

After a minute or so he waved us outside. I thought he was dismissing us, and started to feel angry again, but he followed us into the corridor and closed the door softly.

"You're Armstrong, aren't you? The farmer's son."

"My father's dead, but yes. This is my wife, Katy. "

"Sorry to hear about your father. It's good of you to come. I'm Alex Harper. John's nephew."

I nodded in return. "How is he?"

"Not good, not good at all." He paused. "I feel bad that I haven't visited him before, but I didn't find out until last week."

If he'd been in touch more often, he'd have known that John was ill.

He went on. "This seems kind of tasteless to worry about right now, but, since you're here, would you mind if I took down your address? And… I can't find the key to John's cottage amongst his effects."

Katy smiled. "He never locks the cottage, so he doesn't carry a key."

Alex frowned. "So it's been empty and unsecured all these weeks?" he said.

I shrugged. "It's a farm. There's always somebody about, and the dogs bark at strangers."

"Could you lock it when you get back please, and send me the key?" He passed me two business cards and a pen. Katy scribbled our address on the back on one of them and returned it to him.

"Okay," I said.

"I'd better get back in there," he said. He was waiting for us to leave, I realised.

The car park of the nursing home was laid out in a circle, with a young oak tree on the little island in the middle. As we walked back to the Land Rover I crossed to the tree and laid first my hand and then my forehead on its trunk. The bark was warm in the sun.

"I don't think we'll see him again," I said.

He died that night. The nursing home rang us. Katy cried. I put the spare key to the cottage into a Jiffy bag and addressed it ready to post to Alex Harper in the morning. Then I took our own key and went into the cottage.

I'd visited the place almost every day since John Harper moved in, yet somehow I was seeing it for the first time. It was a stranger's house, now. I felt guilty for being there, even though it was my cottage and there were things here that belonged to Katy and me. I collected them; an old footstool, a desk lamp, a coffee table, some casserole dishes and took them back to the farmhouse.

Then I went to the cottage again. There were piles of sketchbooks on the dresser in the dining room and I knew there were more in the cupboards beneath. I started searching.

Two hours later Katy came out to see where I was.

"It's nearly midnight," she said.

"I can't find it."

She looked at me.

"The Green Man," I said. "I can't find it anywhere."

She bit her lip.

"He promised it to us, Katy, you know he did."

"There are two more bookcases of sketches in the studio," she said.

"I know."

She thought. "Sort them into piles so that you know where you've got to, and come to bed."

But in the morning, before I'd even posted the spare key, Alex Harper was there with a large van and two helpers.

"Morning, Armstrong," he said. "Better get started." To be fair, he didn't sound cheerful about it. "Is there anything of yours left in the cottage?"

"Just the big furniture, and the rug in the living room. I had a look round and took a few other bits last night. I'd lent him a coffee table, that kind of thing."

Harper nodded, and went into the cottage. He came straight out again.

"Have you been messing with his books?"

"John promised us a picture, as a wedding present, but he never gave it to us. I was trying to find it. It's a drawing of me. Kind of."

Harper frowned. "Oh. I see. Well, if it's in the will, you'll get it." He went back into the cottage. I heard him say to one of his men "Good thing we got here quickly, by the look of it."

That was when I started to feel angry.

We weren't invited to the funeral, but we turned up anyway. The vicar told us when it was. We both cried, along with John's agent, but I don't think anyone else did.

A few days later, Alex Harper came up to the farm to clear the last few bits and pieces of John's effects. The only thing left of him was his printing press.

Alex told me that John had left me some money in his will, but not a picture. I tried to be polite and even offered to buy the sketch.

"Sorry, Armstrong," he said, "but I'm afraid I don't think you could afford it. Anyway, nothing's for sale. Not been catalogued yet."

I didn't believe him.

I rang him and left messages, I wrote to him, but heard nothing more. Eight weeks after John had died we got a cheque from the solicitors. The letter didn't mention our appeals for the sketch.

"Leave it," said Katy. "It's not worth it."

"But John promised." Even I could hear how childish I sounded.

"We need the money more," she said. "I think you forgot to spray the bottom field, at any rate the whole lot's black with blight, and... we need to decorate a nursery."

"A what?" I saw the smile growing on her face. "Oh Katy! Are you sure?"

"Yes, I've seen the doctor. Due August 8th."

I counted on my fingers. "So you're nearly three months gone? And you didn't tell me?"

"I didn't realise straight away. I thought I felt ill and tired because of, well, John."

I hugged her. "A baby," I said.

A week later Katy woke bleeding and in pain. She'd lost the baby. It had begun.

Slowly, inevitably, life fell apart. Katy lost two more pregnancies. There was a drought, and then a flood. Crops failed, animals died. We borrowed money, then borrowed money again. Interest rates were high. Katy got a new job, at an office in the town, but she was always tired and I worried about her all the time.

One day I caught sight of myself in the mirror and realised that my face was thin and I was losing my hair. I didn't look like the Green Man any more. I looked like an old man. I was twenty-seven.

In January, 1987, Katy grew pale, and quiet, I kept asking her what was wrong. Was she angry with me? Was she ill? Eventually she gave in.

"I'm pregnant."

I didn't know what to say. I didn't know whether to be happy or not.

"I wasn't going to tell anybody yet. Not till…"

I understood. "I won't tell anyone."

We waited. Kate began to look healthier again, then to show a bump. We'd got past the three month danger period. Slowly we began to admit to other people that she was expecting.

We didn't dare choose baby things, but we walked hand in hand again, and it made it easy to forget the mortgage, and the loan, and the problem with the stream which had somehow become contaminated with iron.

She carried the baby to term, and then… and then… I stay away from that memory. It doesn't happen any more. Mothers don't die in childbed, with their babies blue and still beside them. It doesn't happen.

Katy and our son were cremated. I couldn't afford to have her buried beside my parents in the churchyard. I couldn't afford anything. Andrew drove me home from the funeral. I wouldn't let him come up to the farmhouse. He dropped me at the gate, and I wandered back up through the fields. It had rained all summer; the wheat was mildewed and half the cows had foot rot. Milk yields were down.

Even the barn was at the point of collapse. I walked right up to the door, and ran my fingers over the gouged oak. I remembered Andrew's painting of the Green Man, and John drawing me with Katy watching at his side. I realised that I couldn't live there any more. The land didn't want me.

I declared myself bankrupt, sold the farm and moved to the city. I live in a rented flat and I work for a builder. I watch the football on TV and I go to the pub. I don't talk much and I don't remember and I don't have pets. I don't buy house plants any more.

But on days like today when I can't help remembering, on the days when Katy haunts me, and the fields and the farm lie so heavily around me that I can't see where I am, I go to the City Gallery.

There is one glass case containing work by John Harper. I look at my reflection. I am old and weather-beaten and bald. But if I peer through the reflection and I can see it. Portrait of a Farmer, with Leaves, 1985. A pencil drawing of a man with my face. His hair is a mane of oak leaves and a single oak leaf forms his tongue. He is strong, and young, and ancient. He is life, harvest and rebirth.

And he was taken from me.

Jackie Hawkins

Jackie Hawkins was born in Surrey but has lived in Cambridge since student days. Her first career was in human genetics and she spent several years researching mutations in leukaemia. A career break brought a change in direction and she combined her lifelong interest in both storytelling and the visual arts through studying for a BA in Illustration at the Cambridge School of Art.

Jackie has been writing fiction since the age of five and is currently working on a young adult novel. She had a short story included in the anthology *Music for Another World* and was a finalist in the 2012 Askance competition with *Future Perfect*.

Amongst her other interests Jackie includes gardening, keeping chickens, and training rescue dogs.

Home is Where the Heart (of Darkness) Is
Catherine E Byfield

Picture an ordinary semi-detached house in an ordinary street. A car in the driveway, a mountain bike leaning against the garage door, a row of bedraggled pansies under the front window. Approach the front door (yes, it's a little overdue for a paint job) and hear the noise of a vacuum cleaner competing with the dog's barking and a shouting match between my son and my daughter, which began over possession of the remote control and now includes their dating habits, dress senses and physical appearances (the latter being a rather futile exercise for almost-identical twins).

In short, all the signs of a fairly average family in an average home. Got the picture? Good. Now forget it.

Well, nearly all of it.

For one thing, we don't have a dog. I was learning to ignore such trifles. At least this canine-shaped creature, which had been with us for about three days, was clean, apparently house-trained and didn't shed hairs – mostly because its sinuous body was covered in scales rather than fur.

I turned off the vacuum cleaner and listened as the twins' altercation grew louder, debated yelling at them to put a lid on it. But I'd developed a tolerance for this form of sibling dynamics and learned not to intervene too often in such exchanges. Besides, they'd both reached the creative stage; 'slob's tonsil' was a new epithet on my daughter's part, and a corner of my mind applauded her for it.

My children entered the lounge, followed by the dog (predictably named Griffin by my daughter). I glanced at the creature, noting its, well, lack of substance. None of these chimeras lasted more than a few days. This one, I thought, had only an hour or two at most before its disappearance. Demise? Exorcism?

The first time it had happened, I'd freaked. So had the twins. Anyone would, admit it, when faced with a cross between a harpy and a humming-bird, measuring six inches from snout to tail, appearing in mid-air over the breakfast table, screaming with all the power of its minuscule lungs.

While we sat there, shocked into immobility, two things happened. The toaster launched its payload of bread and the creature squawked in alarm at the sound and hurled itself at my daughter, wrapping its knobby tail around her forearm and chittering in a tone that clearly pleaded for reassurance.

None of us had grasped the connection between it and the garage door.

We were all so shocked that – bar the initial (and inarticulate) exclamations – we didn't talk about the creature. A day or so later I noticed a couple of books on collective conscious and unconscious lying on the desk in my daughter's bedroom, but I didn't mention that either. Nor that the creature grew progressively less substantial over the following days, until it was little more than mist that finally evaporated in a patch of sunlight coming through the kitchen window.

A week later came the second visitation, more problematic this time than a miniature pterodactyl. It's not easy to step around a centaur when it takes up residence in your hallway. On the whole the creature was fairly inoffensive: its diet, far from consisting of nubile virgins in the form of my fifteen-year-old daughter, seemed to be non-existent; and its most threatening gesture was the continual scratching of a tangled mane, and a habit of watching my daughter whenever she was in view.

It took a while for the penny to drop. My daughter had originally claimed the garage for a daunting assembly of drums and a bass guitar or two, and had saved her money over a couple of summers to make the space habitable. My son and I had the wits to recognise the garage as sovereign territory and left her alone to get on with it. So neither of us had been in there for a few months.

Not even when the third visitation banged its head on the garage door frame.

This time I'd seen my daughter emerging through the connecting door between the garage and the kitchen. That wasn't, however, why I dropped the last unchipped soup bowl of Gran's second-best set of Derby porcelain. It was the sight of the thing that followed her.

I defy anyone to confront a cyclops with even a gram of equanimity.

My daughter interpreted my expression pretty accurately, and looked behind her. "Uh oh."

It was on the tip of my tongue to ask her what the hell she'd been up to in the garage, then I realised the idiocy of my reaction. Besides, she was just as flummoxed as I was. But I had to know. I just had to.

I pushed past her, the compulsion over-riding any consideration that I was also elbowing aside half a ton of muscled troglodyte with a single eye in its forehead, and reached out for the door handle.

My daughter grabbed my arm and pulled it away.

"I wouldn't do that, Mum. Besides, there's nothing to see."

"What do you mean, nothing?"

"Really nothing. Trust me." She looked me right in the eye (she hadn't yet outgrown my respectable five foot five). "Right now there is literally nothing. A kind of, I don't know, void or something."

She seemed to have mislaid her usual command of metaphor, but I got the message.

I turned away from the door and wobbled into a chair. My tongue was choked with a myriad responses, from I do not believe this (only, unfortunately, I had to, with the cyclops peering at the top of my daughter's head) to how on earth are we going to feed the thing? (so irrelevant – and wimpish – I couldn't bring myself to say it). My daughter got straight to the point.

"I don't know how it happens, Mum, I really don't. Most of the time everything's okay. But sometimes… well, it's like my head's become a doorway, sort of, and things get out. Or maybe the inside of the garage is, like, the inside of my head. I don't know."

I just gaped at her.

"I'd stop it if I could, honest. But I don't know how it started, so…"

I somehow summoned up a rudimentary power of speech. "Okay, okay. Rats and gargoyles. Just do something with this one. See if you can settle it in a corner or something. Maybe it'll be like the others and fade away."

"Okay. Mum. I'm really…" she looked all of a sudden very young and perplexed, "… okay."

Well, that's how it goes. From time to time these things appear – thankfully, only one at any given time. I did wonder what would happen if one of them materialised in the space one of us was occupying. I grappled with the laws of physics and the undeniable – and incomprehensible – corporeal presence of these creatures, but eventually gave up the attempt. It made my head hurt. And no, we weren't stupid enough to carry on using the garage; but that didn't seem to make a blind bit of difference. The creatures would simply appear, and hover or crouch or flop or slither according to their shape and nature, and within a few days pull a Cheshire cat routine and life would be… normal?

Strangely (and fortunately) it never happened when anyone else was around (can you imagine trying to explain a centaur to the postman?). I even entertained flashes of gratitude to the things for – did I really believe they possessed a degree of tact? Oh what the hell. They didn't often make the kind of noise I had trouble explaining to our neighbours, and they never ate anything; and despite the ferocious appearance of some of the creatures, none of them ever broke, chewed or scratched the furniture or us.

Mind you, we all became fairly well-informed about concepts like collective myth, racial memory, teenage angst, poltergeist phenomena and demon possession. None of which fit the bill, really.

So now the car stays in the drive, and my daughter's become strangely reluctant to keep up with the drum practice. We don't scream any more at the bizarre materialisations. We've even been known to pick up one of the creatures – size and degree of solidity permitting – and dump it in a corner when it interfered with the housework. But late at night I think dark thoughts about adolescent neuroses, wonder sometimes about the heavy metal lyrics my daughter used to blast at the garage walls, and take out my worries and frustrations on a luckless feather pillow.

What if this starts happening to my son? I mean, twins often undergo similar experiences, right? What if his bedroom turns into a void or a vortex or whatever? (I soon stomped on that idea. One inter-dimensional void in my home is enough.)

What happens when my daughter moves out? Goes to college or gets a place of her own? What if this other-dimensional feature of the garage goes with her?

What if it doesn't?

Catherine E. Byfield

Catherine E. Byfield was born in Ohio, USA and moved to the UK in 1978. She is a graduate of Lucy Cavendish College, Cambridge, where she read Anglo-Saxon, Norse and Celtic. Her main scholarly interest is Medieval Welsh dialogue literature. Publications include a study of the Pedeir Keinc y Mabinogi, and Welsh translations of the Ioca Monachorum (co-authored with Martha J. Bayless.)

She is currently preparing editions and translations of four Medieval Welsh texts, with critical commentary, while writing poetry and short stories, and working on her first novel.

In Judith Veritas
MV Blake

Morning
Daniel picked up the knife and fork and stared at them for a moment. Sunlight reflected sharp rays across his vision to rest on the wall. He twisted the silver knife a fraction and the light leapt about, gracefully soaring before reaching a door and rejoining its parent. Daniel smiled and looked back to his breakfast. Sausage. Judith was spoiling him again. She'd even got those fancy sausages from the butchers; filled with herbs and coarse meat, not sawdust and lips. He cut off a section and raised it to his mouth.

"It's not true."

Daniel lowered the piece of sausage and turned to stare at her. "What's not true?"

"When I called you fat. I didn't mean it." Judith strode about, adjusting her hair on the fly.

"When did you call me fat?" Daniel put down the fork and frowned. Judith wandered around, hunting for shoes.

"Last night when you were going to sleep." Her voice came back muffled as she rooted out of sight. "Ah, got you!" she exclaimed.

"You found them?"

"Yeah, they're a bit bent out of shape but I'll soon change that."

"You could always buy new ones?" Daniel went to raise the fork again, his mouth filling with saliva. Judith came back clutching a pair of black dolly shoes and he stopped again.

"You look lovely," he said and smiled at her.

"I know." She grinned happily at him. "Are you going to eat that? I spent ages hunting for them."

Daniel looked down guiltily at his fork and his smile faltered for a brief second. "I suppose I am."

"I'll have it if you don't want it?" Judith started to move towards his breakfast.

Daniel hurriedly popped the meat into his mouth and swallowed it whole.

"Git."

Afternoon

Birds pin-wheeled across the sky, free and graceful, dancing in huge arcs as they swept through the air. Daniel watched their delicate whirls for a while, enjoying the spectacle. He tried to identify some of the birds, but they all looked like pigeons to him. He was never an expert anyway so it came as no surprise. Maybe they were doves. He read once that dove and pigeon were the same thing, or at least white pigeons were doves, or was it smaller ones? He couldn't remember. He killed some time while Judith dozed, counting the white pigeons he saw. There weren't many.

It was about two in the afternoon. He thought it was two anyway. His blasted watch had stopped again. He frowned. He really ought to get the damn thing fixed. Maybe tomorrow. It's too nice a day for such things, he thought. The sun was riding high in the sky and he was starting to feel too gloomy in the shade.

He wandered back to the bed and gently nudged Judith, who grunted and sat bolt upright. She rubbed her eyes and looked around blearily.

"What's up?" she said.

"I fancy a walk. Would you care to join me, my lady?" Judith blinked at him in surprise, and then she smiled.

"If you like, my handsome fellow," she replied. Daniel laughed and helped her up.

"Ready?" he asked. Judith held out her arm and Daniel took it.

"Ready," she said.

Arm in arm, they left their home and began to walk through the streets of London, enjoying the fine day and each other's company. As they walked, they chatted. Daniel would point out areas of interest and Judith would listen avidly as he regaled her of old places and the history of the city. They came to corner of Commercial Street and Whitechapel High Street, and Daniel told her the story of Jack the Ripper and the Whitechapel murders but Judith evidently didn't like to hear about it as she kept squeezing him during the scarier elements.

They walked past Aldgate and down towards Fenchurch Street Station, Daniel portraying every inch the knowledgeable gentleman, pointing out the layered architecture and explaining to Judith that this was the result of the initial station construction, where the buildings and platforms were constructed above Crutched Friars and Savage Gardens. They past underneath the platforms and stopped at St Olave, and Daniel described how the church was originally gutted by Nazi bombs in the Blitz but they restored it. Judith was delighted and puzzled to hear how Norway's King Haakon VII presided over the laying of the new foundations.

"Why a Norwegian king? Why not the Queen?" she asked, frowning up at Daniel's face as he paused in his expository.

"Well, it's Saint Olave isn't it," he said, frowning up at the diminutive church. "He was King Olaf and he fought here against the Danes before the conquest. They built the church as a dedication."

"What's a Norwegian king doing fighting in London? Funny place to find one isn't it?"

"Well, he was mates with the Saxon king at the time. Ethelred I think."

"That explains it I suppose." She looked up at the building. "It's a bit small isn't it?"

"I suppose it is. Still, it's nice they do their soup kitchen on a Saturday. Plenty of folk need that around here."

"Right Christian of them," said Judith. Daniel smiled.

As they continued on to Mark Lane, a young woman pushing a buggy accidentally bumped into Daniel as she turned the corner. She was carrying a bag of shopping and it fell to the floor, scattering items over the pavement. She cursed and leant down to pick them up, holding the buggy in one hand and trying to usher the items into the bag with the other.

"Let me help you dear," said Daniel and he began to kneel down.

"No, it's quite okay, honestly. It was my fault, should have watched where I was going." She began to move more frantically, as if in embarrassment, shoving the shopping roughly in the bag. Her eyes seemed all of a sudden wary, even frightened.

"No, please, I was just as much to blame." Daniel reached for an orange that had spilled from its polythene bag.

"No!" the girl exclaimed. Daniel stopped and stood up. "It's fine," she said, not looking at him. "Just be on your way, thank you."

Daniel frowned and went to reply, but a car was moving slowly up the lane and Judith tugged at his arm to pull him away.

"Well, I never…" he said as they strolled briskly around the corner. Daniel looked back at the woman but she was gone. The orange lay on the floor untouched. "I was only trying to help."

"She left her orange. Maybe she forgot it, we could…" Judith started to turn back, but Daniel stopped her.

"Leave it," he snapped. Judith looked at him and a worried look darted from her eyes.

"Okay Danny, if that's what you want." She shrugged and turned back towards him, placing both of her hands on his. She smiled tentatively at him. Daniel took a deep breath and calmed down somewhat. He laughed shakily.

"Silly to get angry I suppose." He smiled at her sheepishly. "Shall we continue?" Judith held out her arm and they continued their walk.

It was getting late in the afternoon by the time they reached Westminster and Daniel's feet were starting to ache. Judith also looked tired and every step she took seemed to cause her to wince.

"Maybe we should head back. It's getting late and home is calling," said Daniel, looking at Judith in concern. She gave him a look tinged with knowing sadness.

"Why do you do this to yourself?"

"Do what?" Daniel feigned confusion. Judith sighed.

"Sure," she said. "Can we get a bus? My feet are killing me. Maybe these shoes weren't such a good idea."

Daniel thought about it for a moment then nodded. "Anything for you dear," he said with aplomb. "Have we any money? I appear to have left the house without my wallet." Judith laughed loudly at this and began to theatrically hunt through her coat.

"Oh dear, I appear to have left my purse on the kitchen table."

"Well perhaps a passer-by might help us in our hour of need. I hate to beg but someone might take pity on our plight." He adjusted the cuffs of his coat and took on an elite air. "Wait here my dear, I shall attempt to gather us finance." Judith sat down on the steps by Nelson Mandela's statue to rest her feet as Daniel drifted over to a local bus stop.

There were a number of people waiting, but none would look him in the eye. He stopped in front of a young man with ear phones in. He was dressed all in black and the music from his stereo was too loud. The man pulled out an earphone as Daniel approached, a look of apprehension on his face.

"Hello," said Daniel. "I appear to have left my wallet at home and my friend is very tired. Can you spare a little change so we can get the bus home?"

The man shook his head and looked away, putting his earphone back into place. Daniel glowered slightly and tried the next person, an older gentleman than the last. The man didn't even look at him.

Daniel felt a tug on his sleeve. An old lady held out a ten pound note and placed it in Daniel's hand.

"There you go love. Get yourself something nice to eat with that." Daniel looked the old lady in the face and, for a moment, he felt ashamed. For a moment.

"Thank you very much; you are a blessing and no mistake, but it's not for food, we need to get the bus," he said, tucking the note up his sleeve.

"Of course dear, Jesus is with you." The lady smiled and sat down on the bus-stop bench as Daniel walked back to Judith, who had been watching.

"What did she give you?" she asked.

"Enough for the bus at any rate. What a lovely old lady."

"But how much?" She seemed surprisingly earnest. Daniel took her arms and smiled.

"Come on, it doesn't matter. Let's go home."

"Sure." Judith took his hand. "Home."

Evening

By the time it was dark, the warmth of the day had disappeared to be replaced by a nagging cold which caught under their clothes and caused their bones to ache. They cuddled up together, relishing each other's heat through their various layers. Their home was dark and the early moonlight picked out slivers of detail in the darkness. Daniel observed the soft curves of Judith's profile against a silver white background, hiding and accentuating in equal measure. He raised a hand and softly stroked her cheek. He felt her smile fill his palm and she shuffled closer to him, hugging him close.

"My lovely man," she said and sighed again. "This is nice. Snuggly."

Daniel stayed silent and squeezed her waist in reply. He felt warm, even content, and his troubles of the day faded in the quiet bliss of the moment. He started to doze gently.

"Daniel?" Judith's voice seemed disembodied in the dark. Daniel yawned sleepily.

"Yes love?"

"How did you know all that stuff?"

"What stuff?" he replied.

"You know, about the buildings and London and all that about that Danish King."

"Norwegian," he lazily corrected, only half listening really.

"Norwegian King." She turned her body into his to stare at his illuminated face in the moonlight. Her silhouette laid gentle hills of black, edged in silver thread, across his vision.

Daniel took a moment to gather his sleep-scattered thoughts before replying.

"I used to read all the time. I had this idea I suppose that the more I knew, the more I would find my place in the world. Silly I know."

"Did you learn this at school?"

"No, I went to University."

"You went to University? You never told me that!" she exclaimed, gently thumping him on the shoulder.

"Oh yes, studied History for three years at Queen Mary's."

"They teach you about Norwegian Kings at Queen Mary's?"

Daniel laughed softly. "No, it was nothing like that. I picked that stuff up in my own time. I spent most of my youth in the library, reading up on local histories. I used to live round here, so I wanted to know the area, you know, what happened and when."

Judith frowned. "So what did they teach you at University then?"

"It was more about themes in history in specific periods. I ended up knowing a great deal about medieval England I can tell you that much." Daniel yawned.

"Was it useful?" asked Judith.

"Not especially. I think I picked the wrong course." He shrugged.

"Still, you're very clever."

"Evidently so my dear, look where it's got me."

"I'm serious!" she said.

"Well, I suppose I know a lot about specific things, but that's not the same thing as clever, you understand?"

"Yes I think so," said Judith, who didn't. She let out a shiver.

"You want more covers?" asked Daniel.

"No, more cuddles. I'm sleepy. It's been a good day. Goodnight my silly boy."

"Goodnight my dear," said Daniel. Judith turned over to her side and soon fell fast asleep. Daniel stayed awake for a while longer, a sad and wistful smile on his face as he stared at her in the moonlight.

Night

Daniel woke abruptly to find the moon had long since departed to be replaced by dark clouds swollen with rain. He struggled to gather his thoughts together as he sat up. Something had woken him and it wasn't Judith; she was still fast asleep and on her side, a soft and gentle snore passing a quiet refrain into the cold air.

There it was. A noise in the blackness. Daniel carefully pulled away his covers and stood up. It was coming from the doorway. It sounded like boots. Boots of someone trying to walk quietly and failing miserably. A cough, muffled. Daniel's heart began to race, thudding heavily like a drum, so loud in the still silence of his home.

He moved away from the bed, trying not to wake Judith. He crept down the passage to see a shadow in the entrance. That cough again, and the shadow juddered and shrunk in reply.

"Who's there?" he called. The shadow stopped moving, Daniel heard a curse. "Go on; get on with you if you know what's good for you."

The shadow began to retreat, boot steps filling the dead air of the night. Daniel stayed there for a long time after, watching and waiting.

The rain began to fall quietly in the cold dark.

Morning

Judith woke up to find Daniel sitting upright next to her, his face lost in thought as he tapped his fingers together. The sun was just beginning its long race across the sky. Mist formed in the cold air as she yawned.

"Morning Jude. Sleep well?" said Daniel, smiling at her as she stretched out the kinks in her back.

"Like the dead. You must have tired me out yesterday with that walk. I haven't slept that well in years. Why are you awake? It's not like you. Normally I have to kick you to get you moving."

"Ah no reason, just couldn't sleep. Still, I feel wide awake and it looks like it's going to be another nice day." He pushed himself up, shoving off the bedding and jumping about to get some movement back into his muscles. He threw some playful punches in the air.

"Look at you go, Muhammad Bruce Lee. Anyone would think you were happy."

"I'm alright." He grinned at her, then suddenly reached down and picked her up. She squealed as he span her around before hugging her close.

"What's got into you, you silly boy?"

"Just glad to be alive. I feel ready to take on the world," said Daniel, grinning wildly as he let her go.

Judith sighed and started to gather her things. "Still teasing yourself, Danny boy. It won't last forever and it'll hurt more when you let it go. You do know that don't you?"

"I don't know what you're talking about, Jude. It's fine, it really is." The lie passed so easily he barely noticed. Judith shrugged and looked him full in the face. He tried to duck her gaze but she held him in place by her concern.

"Well, you've got me. We'll see each other right," she said, patting him on the cheek affectionately.

Afternoon

Daniel sat on the bench alone, relaxing in the bright sunshine. There was a gentle breeze which provided a pleasant counterpoint to the warmth of the day. The park was glorious; rich green grass grew in neatly confined areas, surrounding trees displaying bright blooms of luxuriant purples and reds. It was quiet and peaceful; not many families with their hordes of unruly children; just young couples in the main, hand in hand, lost in each other's world as they moved slowly across the wide lawns or lounged beneath the shade of the canopies dotted around the greenery.

Judith was working so Daniel had some time to himself. He wished he had a book handy. Maybe tomorrow I'll wander up to St. Pancras and take out a book, I've still got the card somewhere, he thought. I'll have to smarten up a bit.

Someone had left a paper on the bench and he debated about reading that, but he noticed it was a rag tabloid, hardly reading matter, so decided to not bother. Instead he picked it up and dropped it in his shopping bag. Jude might like to read it later, he thought. It'll come in handy anyway.

The birds were out again, racing from tree to tree, their elaborate courtships and games lost on Daniel as he watched. A couple had brought some bread and the birds were beginning to flock around them as they scattered the crumbs clumsily around their feet. The girl kept flinching and yelping if they flew too close and the young man kept laughing at her silly behaviour. Daniel smiled sadly at their antics, remembering when he and his wife did much the same thing. She used to panic if one came within a few feet, and would try to shoo it away with her leg. It never really worked, so she'd eventually hide behind him until he would scatter the crumbs further away from them. She's gone now, he thought sadly. Probably a good thing really, she couldn't cope with this.

But was it really that bad? Daniel didn't think so. Not really. No more bills, no more deadlines, no more disappointments. He was well and truly out of the rat race now. He could do anything he wanted really. It was scary at first, all alone, but Judith was a godsend, and since she came into it all, everything was so much better. He felt almost normal again. Almost.

Maybe if I got a job, he thought. Can't let Jude bring in all the money. Hardly being a gentleman. Yes, a job. He leant forward and put his head in his hands, his brow wrinkled as he debated the reality in his brain. Once I've got enough money, maybe me and Jude could get a place together, a proper home, then maybe we can rebuild what we've lost. She'd like that, he thought. He smiled to himself as his ideas began to take shape.

A couple passed near his bench but gave it a wide berth, the young man keeping a wary eye on him as they went, but Daniel didn't notice. In his mind, he planned an impossible future.

The sun began to dip in the sky, and Daniel was feeling sleepy. He collected his belongings, looked around the park with satisfaction, and then ambled home to wait for Judith.

Evening
Daniel opened his eyes and panicked, as a face leaned over him. It was Judith; she was smiling.

"What the hell do you think you're doing?" he snarled at her, his heart racing. He pushed back the covers and stood up. "You frightened the life out of me!"

"Sorry Danny, but you looked so peaceful dozing like that, it was nice. I didn't mean nothing by it." Her smile fell but she patted him on the arm as a way of apology. Mollified, Daniel put his arms around her and gave her a hug, burying

91

his face in her neck and giving it a kiss. She giggled and batted him away gently.

"None of that my lad." She grinned happily and flung herself down on the bedding. In her hands was a plastic shopping bag.

"What's in the bag?" He slowly lowered himself down to cuddle next to her, relishing her warmth.

"I brought you a snack."

"Really? How did you pay for it? I thought we didn't have any money?" He pushed himself up and broke contact to stare suspiciously at her.

She leant into him conspiratorially. "I found a score in the park while I worked. Must be our lucky day." She beamed and opened the bag, rustling through it happily. Daniel began to smile too.

"So what did you get?" he asked, moving his hand towards the bag. She slapped it sharply, as if batting a playful kitten on the nose.

"Oh, this and that. I don't think you want any of it to be honest, the way you've been carrying on."

"I'm sorry Jude. I didn't mean it. You just startled me, that's all." He assumed a suitably contrite face and gave her an extra squeeze to make sure.

"I don't know…" He could see a small curve to her lips as she carefully tried to hide her smile. He growled at her in mock ferocity and began to tickle her. She giggled happily as she squirmed on the bed. "Stop that!" She squealed. "Stop it you silly man, stop it or you won't have anything." Daniel stopped tickling her immediately, though a few seconds later he sent a warning tickle. She tittered and pushed his hands off.

"Silly boy." She drew the bag up to her lap and smiled at him, her eyes sparkling. Daniel thought it was the most beautiful thing he'd seen in a long time. "Now close your eyes," she said expectantly.

He closed his eyes and a heavy package appeared in his hands. He looked down. It was a sandwich. Not just any sandwich. It advertised a difference. It had more than one type of salad in it. He looked at her.

"For me?" She nodded and smiled; an expression of anxiety and pride on her face.

"You like it?" she asked, doubt spearing her face.

Daniel turned the package around, admiring the food within. He looked up from his inspection.

"I love it," he said.

"There's a drink too." She rummaged through the package and produced a bottle of coke.

"Still my beating heart, my beautiful one," Daniel took the coke and unscrewed the top, taking a long draught of the fizzy liquid. He let out an almighty belch. Judith laughed happily and rummaged some more in the bag. She shyly pulled out a large chocolate bar and showed it to him. When he reached for it she tugged it gently away.

"No, that's for pudding. It's for both of us, halves." She popped the bar back into the bag and pulled out her own sandwich.

"Set to, silly boy, it won't eat itself." Judith chided him, so Daniel wordlessly opened his package and took a big bite, smiling all the while. The crumbs fell down his clothes and onto the bedding but he didn't care. It was a grand day.

Night

He woke with a start as a hand clamped over his mouth. The skin was hard and rough and the stink climbed up his nostrils to pervade his bewildered senses. He kicked out under the bedding but another hand held his thigh. A shadow loomed over his vision and the outline of a face appeared in the moonlight. Rain splattered against the cardboard bedding.

"Stop struggling or I'll gut you and the old bitch," said the dark. Heart pounding, Daniel whimpered and tried to look to his left. He could just see Judith next to him, her crying muffled as another silhouette held her down before a fist smashed into his head, smashing against his cheek and blinding him in one eye. He squealed in pain. Another punch flew; this time in the chest. Daniel struggled to draw in air as he doubled over, heaving into the cold night air.

"Where's the money?" said the dark.

Daniel tried to reply but a clout smashed his head back against the brick wall. He fell on his side, blood pouring from a cut over his eye, wheezing and coughing in agony as rain water puddled against his grimy cheek.

"What… money?" he struggled to release the words.

"The money you and the hag used to buy that grub earlier. We saw you. Now where is it?" A hand whipped out, slow and lazy, and Daniel yelped as the cut above his eye was struck again.

"Joe, do the bitch." Judith cried in agony as the other shadow thumped a huge punch into her gut. Daniel tried to call out in protest but he only managed another whimper before a hand clamped around his throat.

"Now where is it? I won't ask again."

"There… isn't any… more. Don't hurt… her… please."

There was a cry of triumph from Judith's assailant. Daniel and the dark both turned to look. Judith was holding out a black rectangle. It was a wallet.

"How much is in it?" said Joe.

Judith was crying and barely audible, but Joe started to laugh.

"You hear that George? Bitch says there's a bullseye at least!"

"You're kidding?" exclaimed George. "What did they do? Win the lottery? That'll do nicely." He stood up. Daniel tried to turn over, but a boot in the stomach stopped him in his tracks.

"Now don't move, there's a good lad. Pass it here Joe," said George, holding out his hand.

"Don't forget you said we'd go halves," said Joe plaintively. He passed the wallet over. Judith was huddled in a ball, moaning softly.

"I know what I said." George quickly pulled out the notes and dropped the wallet on Daniel's face. His boot was resting on Daniel's stomach. He leant down and grabbed Daniel's chin, pulling his face around to stare into eyes black as coal.

"All a bad dream, mate. Don't get any stupid ideas now, ain't nobody gonna care if I stab you and the bitch up I can promise you." George slapped him playfully across the cheek.

"Come on Joe, let's leave these two lovebirds to it." Daniel felt the boot come off his stomach. He could hear them laughing as they moved off down the alley, the sound of their boots fading into the dark.

Daniel didn't move for some time. The rain had softened, and fell in a gentle shower, washing his face of blood. He blinked when a drop would fall into his eyes. Daniel could hear Judith whimpering next to him, and his chest felt on fire. Slowly, the pain started to recede and he sat up, groaning as his bruised ribs protested against the strain of use. His hands pressed against the cold damp concrete of the alley, grit digging into his palms. The cardboard bedding they had used to stay warm was scattered across the floor, trampled and torn.

"Jude..." he coughed harshly. "Why?"

Judith didn't move, just continued to cry softly to herself. Daniel carefully dragged himself up to his feet, fists clenching and unclenching. He was shaking in anger and fear. He kicked a piece of cardboard across the alley. Judith jumped at the sound, a whine half-formed on her lips.

"God damn it!" cried Daniel. Judith turned over frantically, pawing at his leg.

"Danny, I..." Daniel shook off her hands.

"You lied to me," he said. She raised her smudged and worn face, tears spilling down from her wrinkled eyes.

"I'm sorry Danny, I'm sorry. I was going to tell you about the rest, but I wanted to surprise you." Daniel's face was like a stone, cold, and hard in the night. "You have to believe me, my lovely man, I…"

"Why do I? Why do I have to believe you? I trusted you. If I'd known…" He took a deep shuddering breath. "Go away," he said.

"What…?"

"You heard. Get going. I don't need you." He picked up her bag, her sole belongings, and flung it down the alley towards the street. It made a clatter as her meagre possessions spilled out across the rain-strewn concrete.

"But… this is our home…" she tried and failed. Daniel started to laugh, cruel and dark in the night.

"Home? This isn't a home, this is an alley. Our bed is some damp cardboard I nicked from the supermarket. You work selling street papers to people who won't even look you in the bloody eye. We're unhomed and unwanted, don't you get it? We've got nothing!" The word ripped out of him with all the strength of his grief and pain. "You ruined it all. Now get out!" he screamed, grabbing her and flinging her down the path.

Judith cried out in fear and loss and scrambled her pudgy frame across the passage, tripping over the cardboard, slipping in the wet dark. Daniel threw the bed after her as she escaped his wrath, her frantic footsteps echoing in his ears long after she'd gone.

Morning

The rain stopped before sunrise.

Daniel was huddled under the remnants of the cardboard, shivering in pain and cold. His eye had swollen, blocking his vision on his right side and his head ached from the blows. His clothes were soaked and the cardboard soggy.

The sun breached the horizon, its soft light filling the sky with streaks of red and orange and gold behind retreating rainclouds. He blinked, wincing as his right eyelid tried to mimic its twin. Tears began to spill down his cheeks.

Daniel threw off the cardboard and sat up against the wall, breathing deeply as the tears fell like raindrops, each one carrying a world of anger and pain and loss with it. His rage over Judith dissolved to be replaced by bitter shame over his failures. He pressed his head into his hands and cried. He cried for his house, his job, his life long gone in the wake of his wife's death. He cried for his lost illusions, his belonging, and his place. Most of all, he cried for Judith, his lost soul, old and tired, beaten, abused, betrayed.

He was so lost in his grief he didn't hear the hesitant footsteps. Nor did he see the pudgy smudged hand with its fingerless gloves raise itself up to a mouth bowed in sorrow.

"You silly boy," said Judith, sadly smiling down at him. Daniel looked up; his face a dirty ruin, misery and hope vying with equal weight against his expression.

Judith sat down next to him. "I said it would hurt. What do I know?" She patted him awkwardly on the knee and chuckled.

"Jude..." Daniel tried to speak.

"Hush now, my lovely man, there's nothing to say. I forgive you. The truth is always hard and harder for some than others. But I said we've got each other and I meant it." She put an arm around him and drew him close. She stroked his cheek gently.

"Oh, you're wrong my boy, by the way." She gently pulled his face towards hers and looked him in the eye. "Home is here with me, with you. All we can do is make the best of that. What else can we do?" She smiled at him, and he lost himself in the beauty of that smile.

"Judith?"

"Yes my lovely?"

"Welcome home."

MV Blake

Martin Victor Blake currently resides in Essex, soaking up the ambience of an outer London town with inner city problems. He is currently working as a teacher and has a BSc in Archaeology - digging holes in other people's gardens appeals to his sense of humour. He claims to be much lazier than he appears to be and loves writing short stories. He is currently working on a fantasy novel and says this is mainly so he can childishly relive an infantile desire to be like Conan.

Service Delivery
Simon Humphreys

The road was black and sticky toffee hot as the sun tried to melt the premix surface. A shimmering layer of heat floated knee high, disturbed only by the occasional passing of a soft-drinks truck. There was no wind to move the air, which hung dry and dusty under the cloudless molten white sky. Thandeka's bare feet were as tough as rhino hide having never worn shoes, yet she chose to walk the uneven gravel footpath rather than cook her soles on the smooth, but baking road.

It was not just Thandeka's feet that bore a hardness beyond their years. At barely fifteen, she had long lost the looks deserved of one her age. Slim and petite, with peppercorn hair, her teak toned skin was pimpled and bumpy. She once possessed a beaming smile and sparkling eyes which lit up her face when she giggled and played with the other township children. Her smile was now gone; unseen for months and locked away forever. Her eyes were sad, milky-coffee-coloured and totally bloodshot, lacking hope, revealing nothing and completely emotionless.

She paused to adjust the burden she carried on her back. Bending down, she balanced the baggage, whilst untying the blanket which held it in place. The baggage cried a little, then sporadically whimpered, but sensing the futility, closed her eyelids and gently returned to a place where there was no hunger or pain and mother's breasts were rich with milk. Thandeka tied the knot tight, arched her aching back as much as she could and looked skyward, directly into the blinding sun. Her lips were cracked and parched, but there would be no relief for her thirst until she reached the clinic, some five kilometres on from here. She ran her tongue across her top lip, feeling her way over the roughened surface; catching a flaky, loose piece, which half lifted, half dangled.

It would be another two hours before she reached the clinic; such was the pace of her progress. There was no shade or shelter in the barren landscape and no soothing stream to relieve her swollen feet or cool her salty brow.

She had been walking for an hour and in that time only a handful of vehicles had passed her by. It was too risky to hitch, as there was precious little chance of anyone stopping for a young mother and child, with anything but evil intentions. It had happened before and it would happen again. Lips, noses, eyes and genitals were prized body parts for making "muti" and although never openly discussed in the village, everybody knew of such dangers and feared for the lives of their children.

Thandeka hummed a little tune to relieve the tedium and take her mind off her hunger and thirst, occasionally breaking into song, when her baby began to weep. By mid-afternoon, she had reached the outskirts of the small town and trudged the last few hundred metres up a steep hill to the local clinic, which offered medicine and food to all in need. Being the only clinic in the area, it served a multitude of villages and small townships and there were many in need that day and every day, six days a week.

It was Thandeka's second visit to the clinic with Nomvula, having previously brought her baby there three months ago, when the child was merely six weeks old. On that occasion her grandmother had accompanied her, just to show her the way and to keep an eye on the oldest of six grandchildren in her care. The first journey had seemed far less gruelling and certainly much cooler. This time she felt drained and totally overwhelmed with the whole experience. Nomvula had hardly gained weight in the intervening months, so it was most probably the heat of the day and lack of company which accounted for her exhaustion. Thandeka's grandmother had given her all she could afford, to buy a little food, or in case of emergency. The ten rand she pressed into her granddaughter's fist had been earned from selling little brightly coloured animal beadwork, which was collected from the local women and sold on street corners or the gift shops of big towns and cities far away. Her speciality was miniature lions, about the size of a matchbox, used as key rings or merely hung as ornaments from rear-view mirrors.

The clinic was an old detached house from the 1930s which had been converted. A complete alteration of the original building, combined with a modern extension, courtesy of some much needed Danish Christian aid, had doubled the size of the original dwelling, but totally destroyed any architectural merit which may have existed prior to the conversion.

The long queue which greeted Thandeka and her baby had not been unexpected. A line of forty or more people snaked their way from the entrance door of the Clinic, out onto what had once been a front garden. A haphazard and slow moving queue, which at one point doubled back on itself for no apparent reason, leaving the tale-enders facing the town with their backs to the clinic.

Thandeka didn't really know why she was there. Her grandmother had sent her, saying that Nomvula was not well and needed medicine. The baby was small and cried a lot, but other than that, Thandeka thought she was like all the other babies she had seen in the village.

Thandeka viewed the line of people that twisted like the roadkill cobra she had seen that day... how it resembled that snake she had approached with caution and then kicked into the veld, upon realising it was dead. She hated snakes. Not only was the twisted queue outside the clinic motionless, but it was filled with the old, sick and nearly dead. There were men staring deep down into the ground, bent double with the weight of time, supporting their frail bodies on walking sticks made from branches. A grandmother sat on an upturned beer crate, her grandson holding aloft a black umbrella for shade, barely able to raise it above her head. There were many mothers with babies, just like her own Nomvula; strapped to backs, unable to move.

Thandeka quickened her pace as she passed the queue, not wishing to join it further back than she needed to. First, she needed to drink from the dripping tap on the wall outside a detached block containing two toilets. She lay Nomvula down on the ground next to the brick filled puddle which was a permanent feature below the tap. A dead rat lay nearby giving birth to a family of maggots and a deposit of excrement played host to dozens of swarming flies. She washed her baby's face as best she could and trickled a little liquid into her open mouth with the aid of a cupped hand. Then she placed her head under the tap and ran it full bore, shaking a shower of droplets over her daughter. The water was tepid but so good, as she took her fill directly from the plastic spout of the tap.

Her thirst satisfied, Thandeka strapped her baby to her back once more and walked slowly back past the queue of other mothers, where more flies feasted on streaming noses and swollen eyelids gummed closed with yellow paste.

There she stood, at the tail of a dead snake, not knowing anyone, deep in thought, caring not to waft away insects, nor the demons that welled within, constantly reminding her of that night when against her will, she had been taken into the veld for some "fun". She glanced around once more. There were no such people in her queue that day. Just old men; sad old men... no young men. Good... no young men. She felt glad looking at the sad old men.

Several more people stood in line behind her, as the snake rose from the dead and shuffled a few metres forward, before lapsing once more into a coma. It was painfully slow, but there was no hurry. Thandeka had expected to be sleeping rough that night after the clinic had closed. She would find a safe patch of open ground and cuddle her baby to sleep in a cocoon of body and blanket. But for now, she must be patient and content to be one of the vertebrae in the middle of the snake, moving as the body moves, slowly winding its way towards the clinic.

Thandeka noticed a kindly looking woman, not dissimilar to her own grandmother, walking slowly along the queue from the direction of the clinic. She was talking to all the mothers with babies, taking her time and looking concerned, as if personally involved in the plight of each poor soul waiting their turn. She was a strong woman, who obviously knew about the ways of the world. Her voice was loud, but calm. Perhaps she was a doctor from the clinic, just coming out to see if all was well outside. She caught Thandeka's eye. The young girl looked down instinctively, too shy to hold her ground and not wishing to stare at the clever doctor from the clinic.

The doctor reached Thandeka and paused at the girl's side. She introduced herself as Vumile and told the girl not to worry about her child. The clinic had very good medicine, which would make her baby strong again. She too had a granddaughter Thandeka's age and she was sure that not so long ago she had visited the very village that Thandeka had left that morning.

Vumile chatted for some time and was of great comfort, with her words of wisdom and reassuring manner. She may even have met Thandeka's grandmother on her travels, because when she was told the old lady's name, she immediately remembered meeting someone by that name. It was indeed a very small world and Thandeka apparently reminded Vumile of that lady in so many ways.

There appeared to be a bit more life in the snake, as it slithered ever closer to its destination. But with still some way to go, Thandeka's stomach reminded her that she had not eaten since early that morning and the energy provided by her breakfast of cold mealie pap had been expended hours ago. Nomvula had drunk what breast milk was available, but Thandeka really needed to replenish herself. There was a small Spaza shop some fifty metres away, where she could purchase a loaf of bread and a carton of milk with less than the money she had been given. However she didn't know if the other women would let her re-join the snake if she left now. She didn't know any of them. Perhaps they would turn against her.

Vumile noted her anxiety and offered to take her place in the queue, while she went to fetch food. Thandeka could trust Vumile. She hadn't said she was a doctor from the clinic, but she was kind and friendly. She even knew Thandeka's grandmother.

Vumile said that Thandeka looked tired, which was no surprise, as she'd been carrying Nomvula all day. Her aching bones needed a rest and Vumile suggested the baby be left with her in the queue. She would be quite safe.

Thandeka untied the blanket from around her waist and handed Nomvula and blanket to Vumile. The kind lady eased back the blanket which was partly covering the baby's face and stroked the silky smooth skin with the back of her hand. Vumile cradled the still sleeping infant in her arms and rocked her gently to and fro, whispering a simple lullaby onto the crown of the small child's head. "Tula Tu Tula baba Tula sana."

The bread and milk were bought from the Spaza and Thandeka returned to the snake, instinctively looking along the portion closest to the clinic. She quickly scanned the complete line again from head to toe and back again, quickening her step as the adrenalin pumped through her veins. As she reached the meandering queue of lost souls, she ran to the front, spinning one old lady off her feet as grabbed her shoulder, believing it be that of Vumile. "Eish" the woman cried as she regained her balance.

Thandeka prowled the line, up and down, until she reached the place where she had left her baby. The woman who had been standing behind her stopped her frantic pacing. Within seconds a commotion ensued, as slowly the realisation dawned on the gathering that Vumile had calmly walked away with the baby, as soon as Thandeka had entered the Spaza, Nobody thought anything of it. Surely Thandeka knew her well.

Simon Humphreys

Born in Mursley, Buckinghamshire, in 1956, Simon currently resides in Cape Town, South Africa. He enjoys hockey and spends most weekends sailing.

Having placed his first novel in the pending tray, he's successfully turned his attention to writing short stories. His *Cup of Tea* won first place in a GlobalShortStories.net writing competition, and *Sand Man* featured in the Askance anthology *Positional Vertigo*.

Simon is married and has two teenage children.

The Red Geranium
Sue Dean

It began with a red geranium. Having imagined the geranium into being, she (let's call her the writer) couldn't just leave it. The plant had to have a pot; a ceramic pot, red to match the colour of the geranium. But where was the pot? Sitting on a window sill? Yes, a kitchen window sill. She could see the light streaming through the window setting the geranium on fire.

Neither pot nor geranium had arrived on the window sill unaided. A pair of hands had taken a cutting, dipped it in rooting powder, pushed it into soft earth, had nurtured and watered it as it grew, budded and bloomed. The hands were soft and smooth, a woman's hands. For some time the woman remained unformed; nebulous, dream-like, but the writer's pen couldn't be stilled so the woman who cultivated the red geranium took shape. She was of slim build, blond hair cut in a bob, an unlined face that was open and friendly, a few freckles on a pert nose, a mouth a little too wide perhaps but a mouth that spoke of her generous nature. She certainly didn't look her fifty years. The woman, (Carol was her name, thought the writer) felt the pot on the window sill each day, judging exactly when and how much water it had to have to flourish. She was therefore, careful, nurturing, and methodical.

So, a woman called Carol and a geranium in a pot on a window sill. What about a house, for a window sill cannot exist in isolation? She, the writer, thought some more and gradually constructed a house. It was a square, single storey wooden framed house with a kitchen, bathroom, living room, two bedrooms, a porch, a small garden in the front and a yard at the rear. The writer puzzled for some time over that word 'yard'. Where was the house? It seemed as though it should be in America, possibly Los Angeles? In fact, it looked a little like a house she had once visited, a small, open plan house on a corner lot that had been older and smaller than its bigger and more prosperous neighbours. Was it rented or owned? Rented, the writer decided and then tried to forget the geranium, the woman and the house.

But, they refused to go away. Who was Carol? How had she ended up in Los Angeles in that house? She must have a job. Was it possible that she worked at one of the film or television studios, Fox television perhaps? No, Carol was, the writer decided, an advertising copy writer working for a Hollywood studio; she was good at dreaming up slogans. So Carol has a home and a job but does she live on her own? No, it's not in her nature to be solitary. There is a dog, one of those scruffy, cute ones you see in Disney films. He was a rescue dog, brought home from the dog pound downtown and his name is Scamp. Carol is a conscientious owner and walks Scamp every day. She doesn't over feed him and takes him to the vets for jabs and check-ups when necessary. The dog is as well cared for as the red geranium.

The writer puts down her pen and draws breath. She would like to leave the story there but surely there is more to Carol than just a house, a dog and a geranium? There are her hobbies, her taste in clothes, her way of twisting a lock of her hair around her finger when she is working at her desk. There are her friends, women of her own age and single like her. Why is she single? Well, there was a partner once but after six years of co-habitation he left her for a much younger woman (it's the way in Los Angeles, Carol explains to her friends). She is waiting for a new man to come along and share her life but the world she moves in is full of young, would-be starlets and few available men.

She, the writer, pauses again. Her character, having taken on a life of her own, is not behaving as she should. Carol is looking pensive, frayed around the edges. Something is not right. With a start the writer realises that Carol's life is not going too well. She has lost her job. She is no longer salaried but reduced to doing freelance work and having to pay for her own medical insurance. There is no guarantee of work coming in and Carol has had to use her credit cards and savings to get by. This is not a good place to be and the writer must try to rectify the problem but somehow it can't be done. This story is in danger of heading towards its own inevitable conclusion. The freelance work dries up and Carol is reduced to dog walking and house sitting to make some sort of ends meet.

Why can't Carol go home? The writer calls into being parents and a sibling who might help. But, agh! Carol's parents are old; her father has dementia and her mother a heart condition. They live in St Louis, a place Carol hates, and their house is mortgaged to the bank to pay her parents' medical bills. Besides, Carol's sister is there and she doesn't get on with her sister - a self-righteous, control freak - who would say, "I told you so. Dreams of making it in Hollywood are just that - dreams; and you should have been here, at home all these years, helping to care for our parents."

She, the writer, stops and chews the end of her pen. This story is not going the way she wanted it to at all. She would put the scribbled pages to one side but there is the riddle of the red geranium. So the story will be written and now would be a good time to come up with a happy ending. A handsome advertising executive could come along and rescue Carol but alas, real life intervenes. Such a man does not materialise and Carol, faced with a choice between paying the rent and taking her sick dog to the vets, chooses the dog. She can't pay her credit card bills or her rent and her car quits on her. Things are going from bad to worse. She tries to get unemployment payments but there are endless rules and for reasons Carol can't understand she isn't entitled to anything. The bailiffs come and take away her television, her car (which was not going anywhere anyway) and most of her furniture. And now after all these traumas there must surely be a happy ending?

But, there is still the puzzle of the red geranium and its significance. She, the writer, would like to think that it is a symbol of hope. Her pen hovers. She has the power to do anything but the tale unfolds in its own way. For some stories there cannot be a happy ending.

In Los Angeles on any given night sixty thousand people sleep on the streets. They sleep in bedrolls or in tents, on sidewalks and in parks, mostly in an area of the city called Skid Row. Twenty per cent are war veterans, twenty four per cent are educated to degree standard or above and one of them is Carol. She has a small tent and her meagre belongings in a backpack. Her dog, Scamp, unfortunately died.

And the red geranium? Well, what things are important when all you can own is what you can carry? So, the red geranium in its red pot sticks out of the top of her backpack during the day and is beside her sleeping bag at night. It is the first thing that she sees when she wakes in the mornings.

How does Carol feel about this? Her story is not a conventional one; hardly a Hollywood fairy tale. It's not rags to riches but riches to rags. Carol knows that no one will be interested in her story and she cannot see that it will ever be written.

She, the writer, puts down her pen and closes her notebook.

And now, dear reader, I suppose you will feel cheated. You may have wanted more. You wanted to know everything there was to know about this woman. You wanted to overhear the conversations Carol had with her sister and friends. You wanted to peer into the cracks and crevices of her life and have access to her innermost thoughts. You wanted questions answered. Why did her dog die? How could she be so feckless as to end up on Skid Row? Was there really no hope of a happy ending? What had she done to deserve such a fate?

But you will be disappointed. The writer isn't going to play your game. She knew you wanted not just her sweat but her blood as well and she thinks, quite reasonably, that why should she wear her fingers to the bone just to satisfy your curiosity? Not only has she put down her pen and closed her notebook, but she has left the room, the red geranium but a dim memory that no longer puzzles her. Why?

Well, it was only ever her intention to write a short story about what makes a home a home. Sometimes it can be something as simple as a red geranium.

Sue Dean

Sue Dean has been writing in her spare time since the age of eight. She's had a varied and interesting life and currently combines working full-time running a small music-publishing company with doing a part-time MA in creative writing at Anglia Ruskin University. She lives in a Breckland town on the Suffolk/Norfolk border and refuses to be drawn on how many cats or dogs she shares her life with.

Abandon
Margaret Madeline Loescher

I rise out of the neglected lot like a castle built by a zealous child, one turret and wrap-around porch after another. My windows - hollows for eyes - give away nothing except that weather and time have done their hardest here, the swelling and shrinking of wood. I shed my slates generously. They are stuck at odd angles in the overgrown yard and driveway. I was once a show of wealth in the age of the Mid-Western car manufacturing plants that drew hordes of impoverished workers from the Southern states, the offspring of slaves. They came to the bitter winters, the smoldering shops of metal plates, engine fuel, hard labour under freedom. To show them the dream each corner of this once beautiful façade was elaborated. No one elaborates anymore. Everything must appear smooth as if we lived in an age which no longer confused.

As he comes across my broken porch I can see he's got this way about him: he knows he is heavy and he thinks he is intelligent. Perhaps over time his large shoulders and stomach have grown closer. The stomach lifts, the shoulders curl. His ideas might have come from out of town but his stomach shows he has lived here for many years. He's breathless from the walk from the parked car and up my three stone steps. Is he kind? I search his eyes. Is that not where you find it? They are soft both inside the rim and outside, in the wrinkles that, with age, blend eye with face. He believes in things getting better. He believes in progress through charitable works. (But whose progress?) He eats too much at night, in a darkened kitchen while the dishes drip, drip, drip on to the draining board. I see him now, close, close, close, through the pupil of the front door. This is his moment. He will not be disappointed. I am his chosen mend, his fix. He will renovate.

He knows that by saving me from demolition he will make nothing in the way of dollars, not in this town, but he plays with the idea that it would make him whole again.

My visitor enters with a key. A key! Who has had a key? Many years ago a key was a key. Now the walls are porous, the windows smashed open. No one asks anymore. No one is permitted and no one refused. Behind him is a cop, trussed up, chewing gum, and a real estate agent, weak, slick. No one ever comes to this neighbourhood alone unless you are no one: the chased and tarnished, those for whom harm is an inevitability, done by, done to. The small party stand to attention at the turn of the key. My eye opens, a small, cynical lift of the lid and they pass through.

The smell hits their faces. It is stale, neither dry nor wet, but in between. Something unopened. They laugh in that way that groups of men who do not know each other well laugh: nervously, to make small something that is big. The low pitched guffaw rumbles through the party of three. The policeman adjusts his belt, "Just a lick a paint!" and laughs again, the sound reverberating around the once grand entrance hall, travelling up the ornate staircase shedding many skins of wall paper, to the second floor where the mice stop mid-copulation and tear away across the well trodden boards and into their holes. Someone is here, my little ones! Someone who is someone has arrived!

My visitor stands with his back to the closed door, a sobering look on his fleshy brow. He's looking right up, through the massive gape in the ceiling and to the ceiling of the second floor, original architraves still visible under years of decorating dreams and schemes. He's wondering how such a hole can be mended. He's wondering how such a hole could have been made. He's feeling turned on his head, as if ground and sky were in reverse. He's realizing he hasn't a clue. Then his ego steps in. He is a man who can buy a clue! He's a man who can acquire knowledge, perform authority! His brow stays compressed but he announces,

"Awesome!"

"You said it!" The real estate agent looks under his shoes. He's sure he's stepped in something unsavoury. Then he gestures across the expanse. "Bona fide mansion, my friend."

"This is how they lived!" my visitor begins, "Imagine the carriages pulling up front... coming in here, dressed to the nines! Maybe for a party... Christmas party... the tree – massive tree standing just there-"

"That'd be the spot!" the cop chips in.

"The mingling, live music," he moves towards the staircase and looks up its splintered length to where it disappears into the labyrinth, "the family coming down to greet, the servants coming though from the kitchen – where is the kitchen?"

Carefully, testing boards with toes before their full weight is placed down, they pass from room to room, commenting on fireplaces, doorways. They are looking for something that resembles a kitchen. A room where food was once stored, prepared. What they find is the outside eating its way in. Molds the size of dinner plates hanging from the walls like giant eyes and where there is more light by the sides of windows, ivy enters with its many searching fingers, eating, eating, slowly and resolutely eating. The men do not laugh here. Here they see, silently and unconsciously, how things should be: earth to earth, ashes to ashes, and all that, even for houses. But none admits it, none lets it travel along the neuro pathways to conscious thought for it would ruin everything they ever learnt about progress. They group closer together until they find their way back to the entrance hall.

"Can we?" My visitor gestures towards the upstairs.

"I have," the real estate agent says with hesitation.

"And would you go again?"

"Sure!" He is not but they begin to climb, minus the cop who stands by the door.

"To the left of the stairs the floor is sound. Don't go to the right."

A trapped bird flaps against a pane in a room deep within, a flutter in my heart, but they hear it as the wind or a presence. They do not look at each other. They pause in the hallway just long enough to look into three giant rooms. Rooms where people have been conceived, born, breathed, embraced, coughed and died, and then, quickly,

"Shouldn't we be wearing hard hats?"

He nods and they descend, back out into the winter's day.

Deep in my attic there is a man fast asleep. Inside a paper bag, a cardboard box, and a cupboard, he lies knees to chest, bony arms up to cover his head, almost dead. This is his winter residence. When fall leaves give meaning to a blue sky, I know to expect him. And when the ground turns hard and the winds roll down across the Great Lakes, cutting around my north corner, depositing snow in drifts there, I hear the sound of his shopping cart rattling over the uneven sidewalk slabs like a chain, piled high with bags inside bags inside bags. During the night he parks it in the undergrowth away from the road and, pushing his bad leg in first, lets his thin frame fall through the broken basement window and on to the damp floor, the coal dust of generations smeared across the gloom. He always enters this way, at the bottom and makes his way up my four-story former glory until he comes to his chosen abode: the attic. He has a loping style, his body slowed by the cold, fatigue and age, his lips, dry and broken, moving, ever so slightly moving constantly, the wisps of air through them scented with words. When he reaches the top he finds the remaining cupboard and opens the doors, tapping at the cardboard box inside with his large calloused hands to scare away any mice and then begins to empty the contents of his pockets. The words multiply, still soft, ill-formed, like singing. His hands are busy, unfolding, folding, in and out of pockets, his fingers, stiff and large. Then something is brought to his mouth and eaten. The light fades early up here. In winter one cannot really call it light. Darkness and chill pulls him up and into his bed. A single, dry finger is the last that my attic walls see, as it pulls closed the cupboard door from the inside.

Water drips and freezes until whale-like, the porch a gaping mouth with icicles for baleen bristles, I grin out across the street. Wind finds its way in, whistles round and finds its way out again, taking with it age, disintegrated into dust. There are little pockets of heat: rodents, mushrooms, raccoons in wallpaper nests, and my sometime human resident in his cupboard, heart still beating. Then one day it is warm, hot even and the bats make hay in the rafters. Sirens carry on the breeze. The man climbs out a hole and is gone. I settle and moan. Round and round and round again! Earth to earth, ashes to ashes.

Today it is sweltering summer. The large man with the ideas from out of town and the stomach from round the corner is here again. Today he is alone. Something has changed. He has lost some weight, physical or philosophical. Today he holds something precious. Today he thinks he owns that on which he stands. I can see it in his face as I have seen it on many faces in the past. The key tickles me again. It almost makes me laugh. He holds it with honour, the metal slippery between sweaty thumb and forefinger. He stands on the porch for some time trying it and trying it again. Rubbing it on the fronts of his slacks, and even, with hesitation and look behind him, licking it. Checking his pockets for others. Gently turning the knob as he turns the key, and then gripping the knob, throttling the door, but to no avail. Once a key was a key. Now no one is permitted, no one refused. The exertion has made him sweat. His T-shirt displays a broad, darkening T-shape, the cotton sticking like a second skin. He pulls it free, wipes his brow. For a few minutes he settles himself on the top step of the porch and watches the storm clouds. Rain will come soon, fat drops that hang in the air before they fall. But not before thunder and an electric sky.

He looks at his watch. Perhaps he knows he should not be here too long, not alone. People in this town do crazy things on stormy nights, like horses bucking on the prairie, warning the farmer of tornadoes. He descends the porch steps, starts towards the car and then pauses and turns back. Yes! Something indeed has changed in him! He picks his way through the undergrowth along my east side, using a stick to test the ground through the web of growth. Soon he is burrowing through my backbone, finding footholds, breaking in. Or is it? He thinks it is his! He breaks into himself, braving the sight of decay. Is the kitchen how he remembers it on his last visit? A little older. A little closer to the organic. He does not understand that one day a man, not unlike him will hold it in his hand, a cup of earth, gritty to the touch. And say, "Good spot here. Let's build a house."

A new heart beats within. Someone is here, my little ones! Someone who is someone has arrived! Exhilarated by the effort, the dirt on his hands, he grins wildly, with abandon. And he laughs. Ho! Ho! And he listens to his voice filling the space. He hears it adding to history, being the one on top. And then he begins to climb, moving quickly so as to ride the rush of adrenalin, pushing aside fear. He remembers the real estate agent's caution and at the top of the staircase turns left. He paces through the rooms, endless rooms, touching doorframes, stroking the chipped paint, admiring the years of decorative decisions on the walls, exposed in places like a gently tilting deck of cards. Surely he notices that the day is darkening further? But he is on the stairs to the attic. It is hot up here, and airless. He must feel it, but he does not slow. He fills the space, his mind running, his body perspiring. What does he dream of, here in the attic? I can see from the fierce light in his once soft eyes that he imagines, oh, he imagines! But what is this he sees before him? A last remaining piece of furniture: a broken cupboard. Inside, a cardboard nest, the human stains of sleep, a few worn cloths. He stands back, frightened. Looks about him. The nest feels abandoned.

Now, with sense, he can see that. It is unbearably hot and dark. He should leave but instead he gets down on all fours and pulls the bedding apart. It tears easily. Fine particles of tree pulp and mold spores and human skin puff into the air. It smells like urine. Swearing, he bends over it, stamping it down with his foot. He has started to clear. First this must go and then there will be space. The renovation, the renewal has started. His face contorts, his eyes are black, twisting with a sudden constricting pain. His lungs pull at the rancid air but bring nothing into his body. He turns wildly. Is there someone there? No one. His lungs pull again. Nothing.

My attic eyes turn away from the dying man and look out into the street below. Squirrels leap about, bothered by fleas, restless like the waiting rain. They tear from tree to tree, swaying the branches gracefully. The leaves large and flat and green, turn like waving hands back at me. The air is still and thick. The first water falls through it, punctuating the dry sidewalk, ending the day.

Margaret Madeline Leoscher

Margaret grew up in the mid-West of America, a place that she does not belong but about which she loves to write. She now lives, writes, tells stories and mothers in Cambridge, England.

Although she has always been a writer, she spent a handful of years making documentary films, teaching photography and film-making. She made the professional move from non-fictional moving image to fictionalized written story though her manuscript, *Return to Paterson* about the poet William Carlos Williams.

Home for Valentine's Day
Hannah Constance

I was only just back in the house, shrugging off my coat and loosening my collar, when I saw Laurie positioned in the doorway in front of me. The doorway between our hall and the sitting room.

He watched me as I stepped fully into the house and shut the front door behind me.

"I'm tired," I said and he simply smiled. Something was different, but I was in no mood to inquire. Instead there was a beat of silence as I took off my shoes and placed them haphazardly on the shoe rack – the toes weren't vertical. Too tired. The silence progressed a little longer, but there was nothing unusual in that.

Laurie, now aware of my reluctance to play the game, spoke. "You've forgotten, haven't you?"

I turned to see that he had not moved. "Yes I must have," I replied. "I don't know what you're talking about, so I must have forgotten."

"There's no shame in that," Laurie was grinning. "No shame at all, love. I wasn't expecting you to remember, so you're alright. You guess what day it is."

"Friday." Laurie stepped back into the sitting room at my response and I stepped after him. "It's Friday the fourteenth."

"That's right – it's Valentine's day! You had forgotten."

"I had," I confirmed.

Sitting room. Laurie ushered me further inside. And I could now see that aspects had changed. The lights were off, candles were lit, and the record player from the far corner of the attic had been taken down and placed on top of the piano. It was playing a record, but I didn't know the song. Through the white archway that led into our dining room, I could see that the long table had been laid with decorations – roses and smaller candles.

"But you haven't." I added.

Laurie's gaze continued to follow me and his smile grew even wider. "You're impressed, aren't you?"

"Yes."

"Don't hide it! You like it."

"I'm not."

"You say you're not the romantic type, but I know you are really. Oh, love!"

Laurie had bought new cushions for the sofas, and he had washed the curtains. Everything smelt like jasmine. "This took you a while." I said, looking at him. "You came back from work... early."

Laurie circled the room like it was a gallery, admiring his work. "In fact I did, yes," he said. "I even had time to make a romantic dinner – just for us two."

Now I was by the archway, surveying the dining room and table. "Dinner?" I echoed.

"Yeah! You're hungry, aren't you?"

"Yes."

"Oh, you're so impressed with me." Laurie spoke with pride. I watched him slide past me, walk the length of the dining room, and disappear through the beaded curtain, that led to our kitchen.

★

After a while I began to dislike the smell of jasmine, but I didn't tell Laurie. And by the time he had returned to the table, carrying the main course with him, I had decided it was better if I never told him.

The meal was placed before me, but as Laurie settled down opposite with his plate, I noticed that he still wore that smile. It was... a sly smile. It said that Laurie had something else planned. And either I could guess or I would end up finding out. But I was tired, so I started to eat.

Laurie, following my lead, also ate. His eyes were fixed. "Is it good?"

"Mm."

"You know what else is good?" Laurie asked. He answered his own question. "Meeting up with old friends. That's good, too."

I did what he wanted and looked up. That big mean sly smile was looking back at me.

"I met someone today, love," Laurie said. "A woman. She said she knew you. Had gone to my building to see Smith, but by chance she ended up at my office."

"What was her name?"

Laurie rocked his head. "I don't remember, love," he said honestly. "But she was a school friend of yours, she said. Knew you in the final year. Mechanics class-..."

My gaze was sightless as I disappeared into my Home and plucked out a memory. "Grace Eubridge."

"Yeah," Laurie chewed and swallowed. "You would remember her, wouldn't you?"

"What do you mean?"

"You're so smart, love," Laurie praised me. "I swear you have an answer for everything. And always in a few seconds. Need a name? Bam. What's the answer? Bam. Do you remember this? Bam. You're so smart."

"Thank you Laurie."

"My little fact machine."

"Thank you Laurie."

"So that's what I want to make this evening about," Laurie announced, raising his glass and looking at me. "About you, darling. You hear about me all the time, but we never get to hear about you."

I copied him, raising my own glass of red wine. Half empty.

"To you, my love! And all the funny things that go on inside your head."

Chink, and then settle. Laurie spilt his drink a little as he placed it back down. There was a pause where neither of us

131

ate. Neither of us talked. He waited to see if I would play his game.

"So. This Grace," Laurie started for me. "Let's start this night about you by talking about her. You remember her very well. And isn't it good that she remembers you?"

"I remember everyone at school," I said. "And Grace is... very smart."

"You remember everyone at school?" Laurie asked, getting up from the table and briefly moving into the sitting room. He was going to change the record.

"Yes." I responded, looking at my food.

"Everyone?" Laurie called from the other room. He clapped eyes on me for a second whilst he produced another record. "That's amazing. And just how do you do that, love?"

I said nothing. The new record started playing and Laurie returned to the table.

Now he was laughing softly to himself. "Maybe I should explain instead... You should have heard the conversation that Grace and I had, love. The strangest! Grace suddenly asks me, how's the home? Puzzled, I tell her our house is fine, tell her we've been in it for three years, actually. To which Grace tells me that she wasn't referring to our actual collective *house*, but *your Home*."

It was now explicit what Laurie wanted to talk about this evening. The smell of jasmine was pungent, but I still said nothing.

Laurie continued. "So now I'm thinking what, do you own some secret place somewhere else? A second house you haven't told me about? But luckily Grace is there to clear that one up! No, no, Grace says to me. And then she explained it. A Home was something that you and Grace made up together in your last year of school. Have I ever heard of the *method of loci*? Grace explains it to me. It's a technique that professional memorisers use. In their heads, they think of a route or a map or a place that they will deposit memories or facts upon. You can make the location up, or it can be real. But the gist of it is that if you imagine this place – if you walk around it and place information in recognisable spots – then technically you can never forget anything. You just have to walk back there and find what you left..."

Laurie paused to drink. I waited.

"What a neat party trick, I say to Grace. But Grace is surprised that I – your long-term boyfriend – have never been acquainted with this Home of yours. Why so? I ask. Because, apparently, it's all you ever talked about with Grace. You became obsessed, she says! When she first came across the idea, you both spent time fashioning and making these Homes in your heads, filling them with all the facts and figures you needed to pass your exams. And that must have paid off well. Just one walk through them and you remember everything you need to know. But Grace tells me that she shrugged off the silly idea right after school had finished. But you, apparently, let this Home of yours grow. The last time Grace spoke to you, well, she says it had been 'the size of your head'. Everything was about your Home. And it wasn't just for your facts. The Home now catered for your entire life. The Home was you."

Pause.

"So I just said that I should bring you to more parties."

Laurie continued to eat. I watched him, quietly. Thinking. I didn't want to play. But, as I knew well, either I would make the move or Laurie would make it for me.

So I said, "Yes."

"Mm?"

"Yes Laurie. I have a Home."

"Oh love. That's really special," he said sweetly. He poured out more wine for us. "How organised. Don't you think it's good when you and I can share things like this, between us? Just us two!"

"Us two." I said.

Laurie, looking satisfied, ate the last portions of the main course as if he had killed it himself. Really, I thought, he had spent a lot of time preparing all of this.

Then Laurie said: "But don't think I'm intruding, love. You're alright."

"You're not, Laurie."

"But isn't it good to know how your lover thinks? I think so. And I'm jealous, darling. I really am. I wish I was as structured as that. Able to remember anything, from just a walkabout? Oh, the parties!"

He stood up and cleared the plates. It would soon be time for dessert.

"But love, I won't intrude." Laurie persisted. "I won't, love. It's your night. Me – if I want to remember something, I just chuck it into the dark room that I call my head and just hope to God that I'll find it again when I need it! Scrabble around in the dark! Ha ha! But let's not talk about that any more. Let's change the subject."

Laurie was at the other end of the dining room, and soon slipped out of sight into the kitchen. I could see through the curtain of beads that the silver kitchen counters were messy with preparation. "…But it must be nice for you," he finally said. "It's nice, isn't it?"

Without thinking, I responded. "It's nice. No, it is good."

"Mm?"

I was louder. "It's good. My Home is good, Laurie. It's… beautiful."

Dessert was ready.

★

My glass was half full. The candles – stumps of wax. Jasmine – horrid. But I was talking. "High ceiling. Walls – dark panels of wood that give way to white wallpaper. A faint blue pattern. One central window. Floor to ceiling. Stained glass. It's half masked by the twisting staircase. It's beautiful…"

Our untouched desserts sat in front of us. Melted – neglected.

"What do you keep in there?" Laurie asked.

"In the window, there are etched diagrams of my first aid course, from two years ago. Every stage, so I can always recall it. The stairs have numbers on every step."

"Numbers?"

"Yes. Phone numbers. Bank numbers. Pi digits to eleven decimal places."

Laurie watched me with intense fascination. "Run up the stairs for me."

"3.14159265358."

"Back down."

"85356295141.3."

He laughed. "God – when are you ever going to need to know pi, love?"

"I don't know," I responded. "It might be useful. I can get rid of them. Is it not good?"

"No it's alright. You're alright, darling."

Abruptly, I realised that I was no longer tired. Apart from Grace, this was the first time that I had let anyone else into my Home...

In Laurie's eyes, I could see that he was mapping me out – collecting the spoils for winning the game. "Alright. Isn't this nice? I feel like I'm getting to know you better. But tell me when I'm getting too intrusive, darling. There's always some place that you're not supposed to go!"

"Yes." I drank.

And then Laurie smiled, wide. "I know. A quick game shall finish up the evening. I like games."

"I don't." I suddenly said.

"Oh, my darling fact machine-"

"I don't like jasmine."

"Tell me where you would go... if I told you to define... trite?" He drank. "Yeah. The word trite. Tell me your route through your Home, love."

Laurie's map was as clear as mine.

"East wing," I said. "First floor. From the hall, up the right hand staircase and turn into the first corridor. Go all the way down to the end. Final door. My study. Turn right to view the table with the lamp on it – the bookshelf standing beside it. Its third row. A large red book. Old, rough and thick. The definitions of bizarre words are left here. Trite. An opinion, idea or remark which lacks originality, due to its overuse."

"Amazing!" Laurie cried, standing to take out our ignored dessert bowls. "Oh, and a study. How tidy of you, love. That was fun indeed." He disappeared again for the final time, but still continued to speak to me. "So. That's dinner done, and our game played. What a lovely way to spend Valentine's. Just some quality time. But, tell me love, is there anywhere else that we can go?"

There was no more wine to drink. There was no more music playing. The candles were dying.

"Because, I think there was somewhere else," Laurie pawed. "I think Grace mentioned it to me. She was telling me about some of your stranger rooms – the ones that hold more than just facts. What about those rooms, love?"

Laurie returned to the table, but did not sit down. Instead he clasped the back of his chair firmly, watching me, playing. "Grace tells me a little about them: There'll be rooms for memories, moods, sensations. People. All sorts of things, says Grace. Apparently you did like to talk to Grace about them, love. And that's good. So, I ask Grace, did you have your own room? And Grace responds with, yes, she thinks so. A few. So, you have a few rooms for Grace. Mm? That's interesting. That's alright. It seems that the bigger impression they make on your life, the more space they get in your Home. How very particular of you!"

He moved towards me and I stood up swiftly. "Oh love, happy Valentine's day. Have you enjoyed tonight? Yeah. But I suppose it's getting late. Are you tired now?"

"No."

Laurie nodded. "So am I."

He moved towards me, and I moved back. And again. Again. In these synchronised paces, he moved me out of the dining room and into the sitting room. Out of the sitting room and into the hall. Through the hall and up the stairs.

At the top of the landing, I met a wall.

"Where do you want to go now?" Laurie asked me. His voice was so smooth. Low. "Where can we go from here? A study, a landing. Where do they all lead to, love?"

I knew where he wanted to go. There had been no question asked tonight that Laurie didn't know the answer to. Everything was rhetorical, and everything was planned.

"There is one door," I said. "In my study – there's one door. By my desk. Oak panelled… It leads to my bedroom."

Laurie went to unbutton my jacket, but as I moved sidewards to avoid this, my foot hit a woman's bag. It sat by the bedroom door.

"Shall we go in?" Laurie asked. "To see what's in there? How about it, love?"

"But… you came home from work… early."

"I did," he uttered. "Just for Valentine's Day… Just to see if I could get to know you better. Now, shall we go in?"

"No."

He advanced. "What's in the bedroom, love? Come on. What's to hide? What sorts of facts are stuffed under your mattress? What memories are squeezed behind your wardrobe? What sort of sensation is tucked up in your bed?"

"No." I repeated. "No. No stop! It's empty, Laurie. I do not use the bedroom. It is empty and it is cream coloured and it has chiffon curtains and a carpeted floor and Laurie it is empty…"

"Is it?" I was against the door and he was over me. "But love, isn't it good how we can be so open with each other? So honest! Isn't it good! Happy Valentine's day, love! Let's open the door!"

House and Home became one as Laurie forced open the brown bedroom door with a bang.

There was a pause, but there was nothing unusual in that. Laurie took a moment to survey the empty room. Cream coloured.

"Empty," said Laurie. He strolled around, just to be sure. Then he smiled. "Well, isn't that good, darling?"

"Yes," I said, thinking about the woman that had scuttled under my bed.

Hannah Constance

Hannah Constance was born and raised in Essex, and has an innate passion for acting, drawing and writing. Hannah recently finished her A levels, along with her second novel, and is now studying drama and creative writing at Salford University.

Here story *Home For Valentine's Day* is the first she has entered in a writing competition.

Burrow
Linden Ford

As a child, Frankie had loved stories illustrated by glossy colour plates. His favourite showed a mother squirrel in a frilly apron, baking nut pie. Her kitchen, steam billowing from the oven, was perfectly hidden inside a tree trunk. A few pages further on, two dormice were enjoying a picnic, seated on toadstools, using cups made from acorn-cups.

Frankie longed to climb right inside those pictures. The woodland animals' world looked so sweet and welcoming; he yearned for it so strongly, it almost hurt. Those soft, furry creatures, wearing fine clothes, always chattered together happily. Their bright whiskers quivered as they helped furnish each others' burrows. Pushing moss, leaves, twigs, and found items into place with their velvety snouts, they soon made low-ceilinged warrens and dens look cosy.

It was all so unlike his own suburban home, where outside his bedroom door he heard his stepfather shout and scream harsh, ugly, dangerous words. Frankie wished he could move in with the woodland creatures, snuggled beneath their daintily-embroidered downy quilts, where gentle paws (any sharp claws carefully and lovingly retracted) would tuck him in at night.

The boy grew to be a teenager who loved the countryside and nature. Even just dawdling by an unmown kerbside or a ditch on the way home from school. Or cutting across the recreation ground, although that fenced-off square of sterile grass was too neat and flat for his liking.

He lived mostly for the few summer holidays he had, where there were real fields and cows, and wide skies with birds dancing on the wind.

Somehow, when he left home, Frankie gravitated towards the city. He found a bedsit and lived alone, unhappy or depressed much of the time. When he wasn't working - temp jobs such as stacking shelves - he usually read or watched television, sometimes programmes about country life. But he never thought of going to visit the countryside, and forgot how much he needed it.

One afternoon, trying on jeans in a shop that sold outdoor clothes and camping gear, he was pleased to find the large changing room had been papered from floor to ceiling with an enlarged print of a forest. Frankie chose more clothes to try, just so he could stand among the trees; it was the nearest he'd been to a wood for so long. He inhaled deeply, but the air smelled of nylon and acrylic, and when he touched the bark, he felt only smooth, one-dimensional paper.

Frankie's working life was casual, temporary, unsettled; he found it hard to hold down a job. One of his bosses told him, "You're like a frightened rabbit." Without a regular income, it was hard to pay for his room, but he couldn't go back home to his mother and stepfather and their fights.

He had a few more temp jobs, washing-up at small hotels or restaurants, but the agencies he registered with found him fewer assignments. Eventually, he couldn't keep it all going. He ran out of rent money, and had nowhere to go. Frankie seemed to stand by and watch himself helplessly as he slid into homelessness.

At the hostel, he had a duvet and there were staff to keep an eye on him. But here too there was a lot of shouting outside his door. And for him the modern building had a sealed-in, airless feel. He was grateful for his bed there and all the help he was given; also the camaraderie of his fellow residents. But he longed for a cosy family home with a bit of space.

At last, he was allocated a Council flat, and was so relieved to have his own front door, and no rules. But the building had no soundproofing. He could hear his neighbours turn their lights on and off. And hear everything else they did, even in their bathrooms or bedrooms. There was always somebody's intimate domestic noise all around him.

Upstairs, a young couple, Lenny and Rita, were happily nest-building, making their first home into a haven. They spent Saturdays at the market or shopping arcade, picking out soft furnishings, vases, or unusual objects.

They thought the flats were a great place to live, although they would have liked an extra room. And they were a bit concerned about the new man downstairs who was possibly a bit odd. They had a feeling he could complain about them at the slightest provocation.

They kept the sound down a bit, but weren't going to be dictated to about how they should live in their own home. Anyway, if they tiptoed around now, the man would get used to it and they'd have to keep it up indefinitely. It was just a pity there wasn't more insulation in the flats.

Frankie could identify only too well the night noises coming from the young couple's bed directly above his head. During the day, he tried to work out the other sounds coming from their flat. Was that an exercise bike? A printing press? He trained himself to ignore it all, but sometimes that wasn't possible. He tried turning up his own TV to drown out the noise, but didn't want to disturb his other neighbours.

He began to organise his activities around the couple, maybe do some reading when they were out. But they seemed to do shift work and kept irregular hours, so he couldn't really plan his day. Frankie resented the power they had to dictate his daily timetable. This was his home and shelter; he had a right to live as he wanted. But there was just him, and they were two people together upstairs; he didn't feel able to assert himself.

A local builder gave him a bit of work. Frankie wasn't particularly robust, but he managed it all right. He'd accumulated some decent tools and sometimes did freelance jobs. A woman gardener hired him to help with some of the heavier work such as laying patios.

Apart from these casual connections, he didn't have any regular contact with anyone. He hadn't wanted continued support from the hostel staff, nor to keep in touch with the homeless community. He'd tried to put that part of his life behind him. He wasn't exactly ill either, so didn't have anyone like a social worker.

Lenny and Rita upstairs bought a couple of leaf print cushions, and the spring-like motif inspired them to do more to the flat. Maybe bring a touch of nature indoors. They went to a garden centre in their old car, and brought back a couple of plinths, and two large ferns to go on top of them. Then spent a day repositioning their sofa and chairs so the plants would get enough light. For a fun effect, they spray-painted a fairly small discarded branch they found near the park and planted it in a terracotta container. By the time they'd placed a glass bowl of lemons on the coffee table as a final touch, everything looked really fresh.

Frankie was almost literally climbing the walls. "What are they doing up there, all that scraping about?" And now he had a new next-door neighbour. That thud-thud-thud against his wall for hours must be a dartboard.

None of the neighbours in the block spoke to each other. Frankie wondered if he should contact the young couple or the dart player about the disturbances. But it might make things worse, disrupt the fragile co-operation between them all. Then the others might deliberately make things worse for him.

His flat felt increasingly small and constricting. Sometimes, especially during bad weather on Bank holidays, there seemed no getting away from these strangers so close and all around him. Even the windows of the flats, with their safety catches, didn't let in much air.

In the daytime, if he felt trapped, he might occasionally go to the tiny park. But in the evening, there was no escape. The person next door with the dartboard had a TV now, and

Frankie could hear which programmes were on. It was hopeless to try to read a book.

Lenny and Rita had moved away, given a bigger place when they had a baby; and Frankie had found himself almost missing them. There had been three other couples since then. And now another pair, who had a stereo with a strong bass beat, playing the same track over and again.

One stifling summer evening, restless, Frankie walked around his flat. He stopped and leaned his head against a wall. He could hear everybody's light switches, flushing toilets, footfalls, cutlery, bedsprings, raised voices. He stayed standing there, arms outstretched, palms against the wall.

As he relaxed further into this posture, his body and instincts took over remarkably quickly. Letting his mouth fall open, almost crying out, he breathed deeply. At the same time, he began to push against the smooth plaster with his hands. Beyond this block of flats, he could sense trees, a forest. He imagined freshness, pine needles, resin. All of nature was somewhere out there, and he was absolutely parched.

His open mouth widened into a silent scream as he arched his throat backwards, eyelids squeezed shut. His hands caressed the plaster. Then his fingers were moving like claws, scratching at the hard, resisting wall. He wanted to squeeze himself through the solid surface. His mind's eye filled with trees and vegetation, dark, shiny, leathery leaves with pale veins.

As his feet kicked against the wall, he could feel bracken underfoot, twigs cracking. In his head he heard sweet layers of birdsong coming from the trees and shrubs surrounding him. The air was full of light breezes and gentle rain, rustling and moistening the greenery in all its varied shades. He thirsted, desperate to merge with it all, baring his teeth now in pain and desire.

The earth below him was soft and fragrant. Mother Nature was inviting him in, calling him home. He had to get there, through this unyielding wall, be with her now. He must live untamed, amongst the animals. There arose from his memory an image from an old picture book.

He dug frantically, smashing through what now seemed to be massive tangled knots of tree roots. He was searching for the longed-for burrow, where somehow kind creatures with soft fur would love and cosset him even as he became wild and free. A heavy, gushing rain poured down on his head, like a savage baptism, soaking him.

The young couple had been lying together on the sofa and sat up suddenly. They could hear something and turned down the stereo to listen.

"It's a drill."

Maybe the man downstairs was making some home improvements. Then crashes and bangs, deep thumps. The building was under siege, plaster cracking.

"That's a pickaxe! He's smashing up the wall!"

They ran to the landing as other neighbours appeared. There was water everywhere, ruptured pipes.

"Call the police!"

After that, for a little while Frankie had even less peace and freedom. But at the hospital where he ended up, the grounds were landscaped with flowerbeds. One of the doctors spoke to him about maybe training to be a proper gardener or even a tree surgeon. Or he might start by getting a voluntary job at an animal shelter.

His housing still had to be sorted out, and a social worker was negotiating with the Council. It seemed he might be forgiven. And although the new couple who had lived above him weren't so magnanimous, the dart player (who turned out to be a young woman) had been to see him. She was sorry for any part she'd played in Frankie's story, and came to visit him again.

Frankie sat on a bench in the grounds, drinking coffee with one or two friends he'd made on the ward. Now and then, his mind drifted to the small furry animals who might dwell within the tree trunks at the edge of the grounds.

But increasingly, he allowed himself to imagine a different type of warm, cosy, family scene. This time, one where he felt welcomed by, and at ease with, some kindly human beings.

Linden Ford

After spending some years in Brussels and Paris, Linden Ford returned to England, and currently lives in East Anglia. When in creative mode (which she would like to access more!) she alternates between writing, drawing, and painting and trying to work out what her adopted cat wants for supper.

Homeward
Hugh Kellett

Home. Is it where we start or where we're going?

1936

The Colonel arrived home from riding shortly before the telegram. When it came, it was as terse as it was unexpected, although the Indian boy, peddling up the drive, meandering a little, riding with no hands and whistling, enjoying the scent of jasmine in the air was unaware of the contents of his satchel. He dismounted and propped his bicycle against a palm tree, trotted round the balustrade that marked the end of the verandah, and climbed the steps to the side door, preferring to avoid the front. He pulled on the chain and heard a bell jangle deep inside. A servant answered his call and the envelope, now slightly grubbier than when it began its little journey from Jaipur, was duly handed over. Brushing it down with a cloth, the servant placed it in the silver tray on the mahogany table in the hall and scuttled back through the baize green door. The Colonel's long brown riding boots, slightly dusty, stood sentry-like beside the grandfather clock.

The Colonel, now aged 42, lived, like most soldiers, a life wherever the army took him, of no fixed address, contact being via his club in London or the regimental telegram system. His official home was a flint and stone house, purchased in 1919, on the outskirts of a Wiltshire village changed little since Tudor times. The house was low ceilinged, country-mellow inside with small windows and floral curtains, and was reached via a short gravel path edged with fragrant laurels. He was scarcely a frequent visitor. Prior to this he had lived on and off for the full five years of the Great War in various billets, dug-outs and trenches in northern France, showing considerable valour in the face of peril, leading several raiding parties into enemy trenches and

151

participating in the major battles of the Somme. He knew he was lucky to be alive - wounded five times including a near fatal hit in the head, and had been decorated as a result with the MC and DSO with bar. The majority of his colleagues, young men his equal in valour and dogged enthusiasm, had been less fortunate, and never made it back. At the time, and as a result of this unparalleled blood-letting, he had been temporary Brigadier in the final stages at the age of 24, subsequently demoted in peace time to rank of Captain. Steady postwar progress in various theatres around the world had seen him prosper, becoming Commanding Officer of his beloved Fusilier Battalion, and now, with his fighting days almost over, as a full Colonel attached to the General Staff. A devout, man, he had not planned to be a soldier, having read initially for the Church, but a love of the outdoors and a keen devotion to Country had made him enlist in the Territorial Force a few years ahead of the inevitable outbreak of hostilities and he had simply stayed as a professional when it was all over. The army had made him, and people like him had made the army.

Tall, lean, clipped in all senses of the word, he lived his life in straight lines, or perhaps more accurately, concentric or interlocking circles: God, Country, Empire, Regiment, Family. After the shattering crisis of the early years of the century, these were the foundations around which he confirmed his being. Honour, perhaps more than affection, was his watchword, for who could risk too much in the way of the latter when it had a habit of returning such indulgence with aching disappointment? Did not duty provide a stronger and more useful framework, a commitment to the continuation of things, and a consoling barrier against loss?

That is not to say he did not know or give love, although this was partly a matter of time. Indeed he was not short of admirers. The drain of men and the attraction of his hero status had made him an object of desire for many an upper class English rose and, when in 1921 the arrow finally struck, it struck true. He married a singular example of the species who turned out to be the perfect officer's wife - charming, witty, attentive, understanding of, indeed apparently embracing, the regular domestic upheaval that is the chosen lot of the soldier and his family. Not only this, but, with careful gradualness and sensitivity, she became his head and to an extent his heart, his muse, holding the key to a distant world beyond the confines of the military. From the artificiality, the stiffness, however strong, of convention, she was offering the counterpoint. From a life founded on conquest, one of concord. From the sound of the whistle forcing reluctant men up the trench ladder to the sound of the goatherd's flute on the hillside, or the call of bells in an English village. At times like this, when, in full uniform, he would smoke on the verandah, his tobacco mingling with the tamarind and wild honeysuckle, he would weigh up these thoughts, consider the call and feel the stirrings of a more natural union and of the aching magnetism of home.

The wedding had been in Wiltshire, of course a military affair, with red tunics, medals, brass and steel all a-jingle, and eight brother officers forming a guard of honour, creating a bower of swords for the happy couple to pass under after the service. Later, in the afternoon sunshine, telegrams were received and read out over tea and rock cakes and cucumber sandwiches, including one from the King. Some days later a picture appeared in the London Times.

In quite rapid course, although they were in truth too seldom together in the early years, this marriage bore fruit, four children, three girls to start and then the longed-for boy, born 1929.

Notwithstanding his occasional sentimental lapses for England, the Colonel was happy enough in India. Although part of what was really an occupying force he chose not to see himself as such, and often likened his position, particularly as he no longer bore arms in any meaningful way, as more pastor than soldier. That he enjoyed respect there was no doubt. That he cut a figure even at 42 was not in question. Equally, the fact that he was quietly feared, never struck him as being anything but the natural order of things. He was comfortable, and his immediate surroundings had something of England about them, particularly England in a good summer, when the flowers were in full profusion in the garden. Furniture from home was in quite plentiful evidence too. To this was added more local decorative articles of exoticism such as wild animal skins, elephants' tusks and various Indian metal work and artefacts.

It was a life not without sociability and male comforts. There was the conviviality of the Officers Mess and the senior officers' club, and various dinners, dances and other events to look forward to that the regiment arranged at regular intervals through the year. And of course he could still hunt, usually on horse-back chasing wild pigs, but sometimes by elephant if tigers were the target. Several had already fallen to his marksmanship, their remains adorning wall and floor space.

The Colonel's wife felt less at home in India whenever she visited, which was normally outside the rainy season, but she seldom let on. She developed her hand at landscape painting and involved herself with the local schools, both European and Indian, her soft touch being recognised in the community. The servants seemed to warm to her in a way that would have been unthinkable toward her husband, and, while should would often scold them in a light-hearted way, she would more often be found with them in the kitchen, imparting the secrets of how to bake rock buns and rice pudding.

More for her than for him perhaps was the issue of the children. All four were at boarding schools in England as it had been agreed it was the most constructive way to provide them with stability and grounding, given the itinerant life-style the father's profession entailed. Nevertheless, there was a nagging ache whenever she thought of them locked up in

154

those institutions that smelt so strongly of socks and floor polish, on the other side of the world. The girls, well they were together so to an extent they had each other; but the boy, her last born, what of him aged seven, with his dark good looks? However often he wrote in his effusively cheery letters of how he had done this or won that, they always closed with the same plaintiff ending: When are you coming home, Mummy? These letters she would keep in a box and, when the evening came she could be found stealing quiet reflective moments with them. What if there were another war? The girls would manage but what about the boy, he must not follow the father, luck could, would, simply not last. But then there could never be another war like the last one, she decided. He was safe.

The son had a little box too and in it he kept his collection of die-cast soldiers and other toys, and all his parents' letters. His father's were always to the point, short and regular, usually about animals: we saw this or that snake yesterday or shot this or that creature. They began with the word Dear and were signed with a monogram that his father used, a secret sign between them. This also appeared on the back of the envelope, across the seal, so that the son always knew it was him, as if he needed further clues beyond his handwriting. Often, minor details of the regiment's activities were included, and on one occasion details of such an event were accompanied by a bizarre photograph. It showed the ceremonial beheading of a bullock, with a single stroke of a kukri, by one of the indigenous soldiers of the local battalion. You could see the bullock, tethered in the middle of a parade ground in front of the entire regiment, still standing even though his head had been severed seconds before and now lay before it in the sand. Failure to execute the beast cleanly would mean twelve months' bad luck explained the letter. But how could you still be standing when your head had been removed?

By contrast his mother's letters were long and happy, with a touch of poetry about them, and always began My Dear Darling. They often came accompanied with water colours of beautiful places or stories of the cheeky, light-fingered local Indian boys. While Mummy was incontestably Mummy, the Colonel was just the monogram, personal in its own right but an insignia all the same, a code, with a degree of distance as well as proximity.

The Colonel, reappearing in the hall in stockinged feet eyed the telegram with distrust. Two days previously he had accompanied his wife to the port to embark her safely on the P&O ship Viceroy of India, bound for England via the Suez Canal, a tedious voyage not entirely without risk, but one she had managed several times. She had to see the children. Their parting had been unusually poignant, she talking of when he might be reposted on a permanent basis home in England, he sensing the appeal but not sure where his real duty lay. She spoke of Wiltshire, the children and of the house with its laurel bushes, and whether he might venture the subject with the General; he spoke of unfinished business, but with a look of wistfulness.

She: Can you at least mention it to the top brass or whoever it is? We need to be together, for the children, for us. For the future.

He: We cannot always make our own choices.

There would come a time to settle, to set up home, he said. It would not be long.

As they pushed their way through the quay-side bustle he still looked so fine in his uniform, thought she, and she so, so un-Indian with her understated, beautiful, peaceful mien and slightly enigmatic English pallor, thought he.

She had embarked.

He had waved his swagger stick from the quayside and the Viceroy of India blew its claxon in return, belched a plume of black smoke and departed.

A fly buzzed noisily as he picked up the telegram and moved into the sitting room to read it. He had had occasion to send messages of bleak tidings on countless occasions during the War, and was invariably suspicious of the medium. But in numbed horror he read the following from the purser of the passenger liner:

REGRET TO INFORM YOU COLONEL SIR THAT YOUR WIFE HOMEWARD BOUND FOR ENGLAND ON BOARD THE VICEROY OF INDIA CONTRACTED BLOOD POISONING AND DIED IN THE RED SEA ALMOST OPPOSITE MECCA STOP BURIAL AT SEA HAS ALREADY TAKEN PLACE AS IS THE LOCAL CUSTOM STOP SINCERE CONDOLENCES END

"Will the Colonel be dining in or going to the Club, Sahib?" came a heavily accented Indian voice behind him. There was no answer.

The following day, telegrams were wired by the Colonel to the children, bearing the same unspeakable news, and not altogether more delicately worded. Each was informed of the tragic news by their respective headmaster or mistress. Another memory found itself into the son's box. There was no explanation because it was unexplainable. But the Colonel would be coming home to see them, soon. He was still standing.

1958

The Colonel, noticeably handsome still but having turned prematurely white and lost much of his hair, had returned to England fifteen years previously and had sold the house with the laurels in favour of an altogether grander Elizabethan Hall in Essex farming country. This was partly because he had remarried, after much thought, a family friend and spinster who herself had thrown confetti at his wedding many years before. There were no additional children. A keen gardener, she tended the extensive walled garden of their domain. For his part, he had swapped uniform for baggy corduroys to

157

accommodate his expanding waist-line, and lost himself in his spaniels and his pipe. To the outside world he appeared the image of retired contentment, but he hid a restlessness that travellers of the world never fully lose. Of an evening he would often take the dogs to the highest part of the farm and peer first to westward, to the setting sun and Wiltshire, before swivelling to the East, to the Somme, the Red Sea and beyond to India.

The son, meanwhile, now 29, having failed entry to the Army on medical grounds, had chosen a career in journalism, a profession frowned on by the Colonel, not that he would have exactly acknowledged it as a profession. Previously, and much to the father's chagrin, the son had antagonised the Colonel further by studying, of all subjects, German at Oxford. There had been an unspoken frostiness since that decision which the Colonel had regarded as an act of moral sabotage. They corresponded intermittently, the Colonel still signing with his customary moniker, but the rift, or at least the widening of the gap between them was growing. For the son's part, how could he follow the father's act, upstage the hero? Who was really to blame for the tragedy on the Red Sea? In conversation, when they met, he would struggle with what to call him, settling finally simply on Father, which seemed to suit them both. Yet there were moments of latent longing on both sides for some measure of greater mutual but unachievable intimacy.

It was on one visit to the high point of the farm that the Colonel first felt the headache more acutely than normal and it was only the dogs licking his face as he lay on the ground that brought him round.

The next day the doctors came. The next week the diagnosis. Six months later and the Colonel was dead.

And so it was that his children arrived some days after the cremation to learn of his final wishes. Gathered in the drawing room of the Hall, they drank tea with their step-mother and awaited the arrival of the lawyer.

The will was in a sealed brown envelope that the ancient solicitor, in full morning dress, sweating slightly and wearing an affected pince nez, extracted from his briefcase.

After a few preliminaries, he came to the point. The Colonel had not seen fit to update his will these many years. As a result, it stood written, in plain and incontrovertible black and white and signed by his own hand, that he wished his mortal remains to be cremated and placed, scattered or buried alongside those of his wife, and here the man at law looked somewhat shamefacedly at the stepmother, that is to say his first wife who is hereunder named in person.

Whether this had been a deliberate act of the Colonel or an understandable lapse was a matter of some debate, but a will was a will, and the son, attempting a joke to break the incredulity and embarrassment, ventured that where there was a will there was a way.

And so he found himself in 1958, a man of that lucky age that had watched the second great war of the twentieth century from a safe distance, in an aircraft from London to Cairo and thence to Djibouti, clutching a valise and small urn that had been subject to the quizzical attention of the customs officials at each stop-over.

On arrival at the port he had booked passage across the Red Sea towards Mecca, a crossing of some twenty four hours. It was a sizeable if rather dilapidated steamer with three classes of passenger decks and a restaurant and with entertainment laid on in the evening in the form of the ship's brass band. On leaving Djibouti he had the overwhelming feeling that he was sailing across a major fault line in the surface of the world, that clove East from West, towards a place of some considerable holiness and peace.

After settling in, and about two hours into the voyage, he sought an appointment with the purser, explained his mission, and sought sanction to scatter the ashes to fulfil it. Touched, the purser said he needed to consult with the Captain.

The son waited.

The Captain appeared. Blond, unshaven, open necked, around 40. He played back what the purser had told him, speaking in a heavy German accent:

"So, we have on board the mortal remains of a British army officer?"

The son nodded.

"I was a U-boat commander during the last war, and sunk many ships, but if we have a deceased British officer on board the very least we can do is honour his final journey. This is the fitting way to close."

An hour later and the purser had assembled the ship's band on the aft deck, and the Captain, now cleaned up and uniformed, had informed the passengers and crew as to the peculiar circumstances that they found themselves in.

As the sun dipped he closed down the engines and the ship fell silent, adrift in almost flat calm. The son, clutching the urn and valise was ushered aft to the railings at the stern as the band's French horn player sounded the Last Post. The ship's company saluted as the stars came out and the son, leaning out as far as he could, inverted the urn to release its contents. So fine were the ashes that many blew back on deck carried by a sudden light gust, and landed as small speckles on the son and on the white uniforms of the funeral party.

He opened his valise and extracted a small wreath made of laurels from a Wiltshire village, and threw it into the sea.

It bore one word: HOME.

Is it where we start or where we're going?

24 Hours
Zainab Thamer

I

I stood alone in the airport a little bit after midnight. I crossed the portal for the first time in my life, and I felt immediately that I was in a new world. My passport and ticket were tightly held in my hand. I looked every thirty seconds at my ticket to check my gate number. I was confused and worried. I didn't exactly know why I felt that way, but it was the same feeling I got when I had to take an exam or to speak in front of people. I knew the place was noisy; I could see people talking and dragging their carry-on bags. But honestly, I could only hear the sound of my shoes hitting the ground.

The idea of leaving home distressed me. I didn't know what to expect or whether I could handle being in a strange world. What if I could adjust to them but others couldn't accept me? What if I failed in truly representing myself? I took a deep breath, squeezed the belt of my bag with my fist and kept moving.

I sat by my gate. I checked my ticket again and adjusted my bag. There was a man sitting in front of me. I looked at him and thought of asking him about the flight. No, you checked hundreds of times, it can't be wrong, I thought.

But I couldn't resist my thoughts. I could hear a voice inside my head saying you don't want to miss your flight do you? Do you want to live in the circle of "What if?" Without any delay I said, "Excuse me sir. Is my flight the same as yours?" He was delighted to look at my ticket and told me it was. I was embarrassed, actually, to ask. I knew it was the right gate, and I was positively sure. But this uncertainty inside me drove me insane.

A few minutes later the call for our flight was announced. The man blinked with a small nod and said, "Yes, it's our flight!" I gave him a big smile and went to boarding. I was again embarrassed. He knew I'm a person of doubts. I sank into my thoughts and started to cheer myself up. I'm strong! I can do it on my own. You won't be lost. This is my way to… a phone call interrupted me. I opened my bag and started to dig it up. It was my friend. He called me because he couldn't make it to the airport to say goodbye. He sensed the nervousness in my voice and told me not to worry. "You will definitely find something that reminds you of home." It was the last sentence I heard from home. I held my phone and looked at it, it said the call duration was five minutes and thirty seconds. Why couldn't he make it? He was the one who pushed me to take this trip. "You don't realise how many great things you can achieve in life. Stop being worried and stop questioning your abilities. Let your dreams take you to a place as big as your ambitions." He told me that. He pushed me from a cliff and cut the rope holding me to home.

On my way into the plane, I was just laughing at myself and what had happened to me. Everyone who met me or spoke to me knew that there was something wrong with me. I felt I was in a world of therapists. With every step I took forward, I became more confident. I told myself that it's okay to feel uncertain as a way to comfort myself.

I found my seat in the middle. I was annoyed because I wanted a seat by the window. It didn't bother me that much though. I was overwhelmed by my trip to a new world and it didn't matter as long as I had a seat. I sat and buckled up and started to check out the people around me. It was depressing! Everyone was asleep or trying to. The lights were so soft. The only thing I heard was the sound of whispering. Oh please don't let me suffer this way the whole trip, I said to myself.

It was so quiet. I'd never been in a place as quiet as that before. I looked at the man sitting next to me. He was covered with a blanket and deeply asleep. Why? I thought, I prepared millions of conversations inside my head to share with whoever would sit next to me. I was begging to hear some noises. After a few seconds, a baby started crying. Not this kind of noises! I was so down and didn't know what to do. I felt stuck between earth and sky. I always wanted the chance to leave home and go away, so, I didn't allow myself to think of home or wishing to go back.

I started to get frustrated. I decided to do what everyone did: sleep. I tried to lean back on the seat to the right and then to the left. But I couldn't find a comfortable position. I looked at how others were sleeping. Maybe I could find a good posture to mimic. I looked to my right and to my left. Maybe there are more choices in the back. Maybe I should take a look! I turned to my right, and I started staring at people. An old man looked awkwardly at me. He seemed suspicious as to why I was looking at people that way. Immediately, I pretended that I was looking for someone else. I looked at someone who was sleeping and made a gesture as though I had found who I was looking for. I turned and I felt stupid, but there was a huge smile on my face. I must have watched a lot of movies! Why did I suppose he was looking at me with suspicion? He might be as bored as I was and he was happy to see someone moving besides him. I smiled. Now for sure he would think I'm out of my mind! This last thought made me laugh. First I felt lost and then crazy. What would come next?

I leaned on my right hand and thought of nothing but sleeping. The next thing I remembered was waking up. The man who was sitting next to me mistakenly hit me by his elbow and woke me up. "Sorry," said the man and got back to his sweet dreams. "Sorry" was the first and last word I heard from him. I was confused about the place I was in, because just before he woke me up I was dreaming of home. I was with my family at the airport having dinner. It seemed I kept going back to the last event I had before boarding.

I tried to go back to sleep, but there was no way to do that. I checked the time, and it turned out that I had slept for less than half an hour. I was so frustrated. I looked at the man and thought, thanks a lot, you don't talk, and now you've ruined my sleep. I sighed and relived the same torture I had at the beginning of the flight.

I knew that I might be stuck in boredom during my flight, so I was fully armed. I pulled out my bag containing my notebook and a book. I took the book. It was grey with a big picture of the author. I started to read it with no enthusiasm. Every time I flipped a page, I thought the sound would wake someone. I read ten and a half pages. I underlined a few sentences I liked. But I couldn't keep on. I was forcing myself to read it and enjoy it. I didn't want to kill the words by my lack of imagination.

A paper and a pen would never let me down, I thought. I grabbed my notebook, and searched for a pen, but all I found was a sharp pencil. A pencil would do the job. It had been a while since my fingers touched a pencil. I liked how smoothly and gently my words were delivered. The sound of the pencil I heard while I was writing amused me. I never thought of that sound before. But certainly I felt it was the pencil's way of pronouncing my words with pleasure. After I dried out of ideas, I closed my notebook and returned it. While I was trying to close my bag, the zipper stuck. I tried to find what the problem was. The soft yellow lights didn't help, and every time I tried to look, my own grey shadow swallowed the light. I was about to give up before I noticed something inside the bag; it was a letter. I didn't bring it with me, I'm definitely sure. I took it out; it was the acceptance letter for the summer job I applied for. I remembered when I first received it. I was in class. I was thrilled and wanted to jump all over the place, but I couldn't. The memory made me forget where I was. I felt confidant. Before I closed it, I saw a yellow note. It said, "So proud of you. I know you can do it." It didn't say who wrote it. But I knew it was from my mother. Not because she was the one who packed my bag, but because I could hear her compassionate voice through the words.

The sunbeams broke into my eyes in stripes. I was struggling to refresh my body while the captain was announcing our arrival. I had slept for a few hours, that must be some kind of accomplishment.

On my way out of the plane I felt like a person seeking freedom after a long detention, or like a little kid who was waiting for school to finish in order to go back home. But in my case I wasn't sure if I would find a home.

II

I walked out not knowing what direction to take. I had tens of papers, and all I had to do was follow what they said. I felt I was in a maze; each place led to another. The escalator led me to the corridors; the corridors led to more gates.

I had to go through the security check-in again. On top of all my sufferings, the security woman told me with a frowning face to take my shoes and jacket off. I didn't bother to smile or to respond.

Finding my gate was another story. Once I found a seat, I crashed on it. I had to wait several hours for my next flight. During my previous flight, I felt mute and outcast. The situation in the airport was no better, there was no opportunity for communication.

Normally, I wouldn't sleep, probably. Either there would be future plans to think about, or voices that I would hear and would keep me awake till the morning. So, I wasn't uncomfortable with my situation. Food could keep me busy for a while, I thought. I couldn't eat anything in the plane so I thought of having something big. But all I ended up with was a bottle of water, an orange juice and yoghurt. After all, it was no fun to eat by myself, so my food portion decreased to a small serving.

I couldn't finish my food, and it only took me a few minutes to eat half of it. I felt I was going crazy. I lost my appetite and my ability to sleep. Unbelievable. I didn't know what to do. I was desperately tired. If I could get only one thing from home, it would be with no question, my bed.

It had been hours since I had proper sleep or real food. I had no power, but still, I kept wandering around. I thought maybe, maybe I will find someone I know, or someone to talk to. It would definitely give me some energy to get through this time.

Unfortunately, everyone minded his own affairs. I went here, and there and nobody even bothered to look at me. I squandered millions of smiles and got none in return. Is this a real world?

I thought of going to the bathroom to refresh myself. I pulled some tissues and laid them aside on the floor to put my bag on. I stood in front of the mirror and I looked a bit pale. "Hi, I missed me," I said to myself with a smile. I felt it had been ages since I saw myself, and I felt I forgot how I looked after all I had been through. If not for my grey jacket, I didn't think I would be certain it was me. I turned on the tap and the water was so cold. I started washing my face heavily. My moment of peace was cut by a harsh voice. The voice was tense, and the tone wasn't friendly.

"What do you think you are doing?" said the worker. I didn't know what to say. I started to rethink of what I was doing. Is it possible that because of my lack of sleep I had started to do unnatural things? Things that I couldn't even be aware of?

I said, with hesitation, "Washing my face!"

"No, you are not! You're splashing the floor. Look around you and you'll see the spots," said the worker with an angry tone. She said it as if I had done an unforgivable deed. I was speechless, but I had to answer her so I told her I didn't mean to. I didn't do it deliberately.

The worker left and said, "Yes you did!"

I felt like someone had stabbed me right in the heart. I had no one to tell what had happened. I just needed someone to tell me it was okay and that I would get through it. I needed a pat on my back to comfort my hurt feelings. The whole idea of washing my face became painful. I turned to see where the tissues were. They were right across from me. I headed toward them to dry my face and hands. On my way I heard the same voice again say, "Are you kidding me? Are you trying to make me mad?" I was actually surprised. What have I done this time?

I turned and said, "I'm sorry, what do you mean?"

The worker replied with frustration, "First you splashed the floor, and now you are walking around to drop water all around!"

I couldn't be calm any more. "No, I was not. There are a few drops, and they might not even be mine!" I took my bag and left. I didn't know why the worker was talking to me that way. I didn't know how a person in my position would feel. But I knew that I felt lost. It was not the conversation I was waiting for. Maybe it was better to be quiet and alone after all.

I started my observations again. There was a man reading his newspaper, a boy listening to his music, and then I stopped looking. I was in a world with no communication. The atmosphere was suffocating me and the silence seemed to paralyse their bodies. Maybe that's why they can't smile.

I joined the paralysed group. I started to count how many hours I had spent. Seven hours in the plane, four hours here so far, and still five hours left before I leave! It was an endless nightmare. Out of frustration, I lifted my head and looked to my right. Surprisingly, I saw someone smiling to me. What a miracle! It was a beautiful young girl with blond wavy hair. Her eyes were glowing and her smile was as wide as the world. She was sitting a few seats away from me. With no hesitation, I smiled back and said "Hi!"

She immediately stood up and rushed to sit next to me. "Hi, my name is Nina. How are you?" She was more eager than I was to start a conversation. Her words snatched the lock off my mouth and set my tongue free. I greeted her back. She told me she was from Bulgaria. She asked me whether I knew anything about her country. I wasn't ashamed to say no, because she knew nothing about mine either.

"Don't you find it odd?" she said with a very tender tone.

"What do you mean?" I replied.

She said, "I mean everyone busy doing something. No smile, no talk."

I said to her, "Yes, of course, my friend. I know exactly what are you talking about. I've suffered from this the past half day, and you were the only one who has even looked at me!"

She wasn't surprised. She was nodding and shaking her head, saying yes, yes!

She looked innocently at me and said, "Do you have a hairbrush? I need one but nobody has bothered to look at me. You were the only one who looked at me so I wondered, maybe you have one?"

At that moment I really wished I had one. She was so nice and I didn't want to say no to her. "I'm really sorry, but I don't."

She was a little bit bothered. "I'm meeting my boyfriend," she said. After a short pause, she looked at me and her eyes looked so dreamy and said, "I haven't met him in four months. That is why I asked for a hair brush."

"You look beautiful," I said to her. "You don't need one. It's fine." She smiled and seemed relieved and thanked me.

Not long after that, she looked at her watch and told me it was time for her to leave. It was sad seeing the only good companion leaving, but I could do nothing but accept reality. Once she left, I regretted that I hadn't taken any contact information from her. I was overwhelmed by talking to her and didn't think of asking her about any of that.

I looked at my watch. God it's almost time. I must rush. I went searching for my gate. I walked as fast I as I could to reach the gate. When I reached it, I remembered what happened to me in the other airport. I am still me, I can't change overnight. I need to ask someone if it's my flight. I looked and saw a man. He seemed helpful, just like the one I saw back home. I went to him and asked and he answered me with kindness. I walked around to check the place, but my thoughts wouldn't leave me alone. They pushed me to go back to be near him so I wouldn't miss my flight. When I returned, I didn't see him. I would be lying if I said that I wasn't scared that the plane had left. Nonsense! Where these ideas come from, I thought.

I entered the gate and headed directly to my seat. Another nine hours to my second destination. I sat, buckled up, pulled up the blanket, and covered myself and closed my eyes. Now, I will be the person who spends the whole flight sleeping. No more drama.

III

The plan didn't work. I could only sleep for one hour, and the rest was the same as my previous flight. But I made it to the end. Once we landed, I pushed myself forward, dragging my legs as if they had never been a part of me.

I stood waiting for my luggage. All I saw were big, small, green, black and blue suitcases. I couldn't afford to look at faces any more. I saw my bag coming; I stepped forward and pulled it off the belt. But it was so heavy. "Take a deep breath. One, two and now!" surprisingly, I pulled it down. It was even lighter than my back pack. What strength I have! But when I put it down, I saw a hand on it. I looked up and there was a man who had pulled it for me. He smiled and said, "Here you go!"

I was stunned! People can see me now. It wasn't my fault after all. I was so thrilled that I forgot to thank him. I walked and everyone was smiling and talking. This was the first time in more than 24 hours that I didn't hear my shoes or the voice inside me. I like this world already.

In front of me was the check-in security. I remembered what had happened to me in my previous flight, and I was anxious to step forward. But it wasn't an option. Immediately, the women there said with a very tender tone, "I'm sorry, but do you mind taking off your jacket and shoes?" What a parallel! Is it true, or am I dreaming? She is asking me whether I mind. Why on earth would I?

I had to go through a maze again. But it wasn't so bad. I was an expert by then. I looked down, and I heard a man saying to me, "Do you know where to go?"

"No, but I will now," I said to the man.

He said, "Don't bother yourself," And then started to give me direction to where I should go. I felt I was a ghost in the last airport. But here, I exist. I'm somebody in this world.

Once I arrived to the gates area, I saw a huge glass window covering heaven behind it. There was a beautiful landscape behind that window. The sky was so rich in colour and the trees were all the same height. The clouds were very fluffy and had three dimensions. I wasn't used to these views. I only saw faded colours and naked skies. All the suffering I had been through went away. I was born again.

"Do you like the view?" a voice came from behind. I turned, and it was the man I saw in the previous airport and who I had asked about the flight.

"Hi, again! Yes of course I do! It's so…" I paused for seconds not knowing how to describe the view.

"Relieving?" he said.

"Exactly. Relieving," I replied.

Both of us were standing and facing the huge glass window. I meditated the view. Nature gave me what I had lost during the previous hours: hope.

"You seem so fond of this view. There was the same view in the last airport. Why do you like this view better?" I didn't exactly know what he was talking about. Were we in the same airport? I was trying to think if I knew this man in the first place.

"What view? What are you talking about? I saw nothing," I said to him.

"Well, there was a nice view there as well. But you might have missed it because your mind was busy," said the man.

"Maybe you're right. It wasn't me there after all," I replied to him.

"Well, you have to excuse me now; I have a flight to catch."

"Sure. It was nice meeting you. Farewell."

He left and his sentence couldn't leave my mind. Why couldn't I see the view there? Is it me or was it because of the gloomy atmosphere? It's not me it must be because of people. If they are so hostile, the brightest sun wouldn't come through. Maybe it was the reason why I couldn't see the view.

This time when I went to the ladies room, the lady working there only smiled at me, saying nothing except "hi". I realised why all of that had happened to me: to make me actually value the things I didn't notice. The little help, the small chats, even the smiles and a simple word such as "hi."

I went to a shop to get something to eat. The only thing I craved was a small pack of M&Ms. I put it in my pocket and went out to find a place to enjoy my meal. While I was watching the lively world, I heard the sound of a cleaning trolley approaching me. I turned to my right, and it was the cleaning lady who I had met earlier. She came and sat next to me and said, "You seem very happy. Do you like it here?"

"There is no reason I shouldn't," I said.

"But you haven't seen anything yet. It's only the entrance. The house might look different from the inside," she said to me.

"No, it actually tells a lot. I just know it," I said.

"Why is that?" she asked me.

"The people, the atmosphere, the way people treat me, all of these make me feel like I am at home."

She smiled and put her maternal hand on my shoulder, patted me and left. I was the happiest person on earth.

I checked the clock and was supposed to be boarding. I lined up thinking of all that happened to me. Only then I realised I hadn't asked anyone about the flight. I don't need to ask. I'm positively sure. I remembered the last words I heard from home, about finding things to remind me of it. I realised it was not necessary to find something to remind me of home, but rather a feeling of being welcomed. I realised why we say we feel just like home: because we feel it, not because we see it.

I was rationalising what happened to me while taking my ticket out of my bag when a young man said, "Excuse me, is your flight the same as mine?" I smiled, not believing what I heard. I looked to his ticket, it was folded in half.

"It's the same," I told him. Through his face I could actually see how my face looked in the beginning of my trip. He was uncertain and lost, just as I had been.

It turned out that I could change overnight. For me, it didn't feel like all that happened was only a day. It felt like a lifetime. Now I can sleep, and only now I am not worried about my next destination, I thought, as I merged with the other passengers.

Zainab Thamer

Zainab Thamer is a senior English-language and literature student at the University of Bahrain and has been writing since the age of nine. She mainly writes poetry but has never published any of her work. Sending her story *24 Hours* to Askance was her first submission of any kind.

Zainab has an interest in politics and social improvement and has been selected for two programs in the United States: journalism at the Murrow College, and women's rights at Wheelock College.

In the future Zainab is hoping to do a Masters in Creative Writing in the UK. Her ambitions are wide, with aspirations to be a journalist, a novelist and, perhaps, also a photographer.

When Sister Came Home
Phil Arnold

May, 1960.

Sister was coming home.

Her real name was Elizabeth, but for some reason everyone in our family called her either Sister or Sis and had done so for as long as I could remember. She had been away for almost two years – travelling and working in England and 'on the continent'. Now she was coming home. It had come as a bit of a surprise, because none of her letters had indicated that 'home' was something she even thought about, much less longed to return to. They were full of the excitement of her travels: new places, new faces, new friends and experiences. But they always seemed to imply that 'home' was somehow lesser by comparison.

The telegram had arrived at ten on Monday morning, and lay, unopened, on the hall table all day. There was a certain reverence in our home towards telegrams. Perhaps it was a hangover from the war years when every telegram meant important, if not bad, news of some kind.

So it sat there, propped against the Bakelite telephone, assuming an importance far out of proportion to its size, until Father arrived home for the ceremonial opening that evening.

ARRIVING HOME SATURDAY JUNE 4 QANTAS FLIGHT 416 FROM SINGAPORE STOP LUGGAGE FOLLOWING BY BOAT STOP LOVE ELIZABETH STOP.

There was much excitement. Less than two weeks! Neighbours were invited in, relatives and more distant friends were contacted and told the news. Wasn't it wonderful? How typical of Sister to make such an unexpected decision!

But, as well as generating excitement, the telegram also raised questions. It was Aunty Dolly who, seemingly innocently, sowed the seeds of doubt and anxiety.

"I do hope there's nothing wrong dear," she said, with a tone in her voice and as expression on her face that suggested all sorts of dire possibilities.

Of course there was nothing wrong! There was a defensive, prickly tone in my mother's response that refused to even contemplate the possibility. But why was she coming home so suddenly? The sketchiness of the information fostered conjecture. Had she met someone? Was she well? Had something happened?

And there was a hidden question, which hovered, suggested but unasked, and not even understood by us kids. It was alluded to only by knowing glances and something that Uncle Charlie said that elicited a furtive giggle from cousin Julie, whom my mother had never liked, and a fierce glare from Aunt Sarah.

Aunt Sarah was full of reassurances, but succeeded only in creating an even greater sense of unease which lasted the whole fortnight, and produced frantic, compensatory activity on the part of Mum.

The house was cleaned from floor to ceiling. Curtains were washed, windows cleaned and re-cleaned, floors scrubbed, furniture polished, and carpets vacuumed. I was sent to clean up the yard, weed the garden and help Dad tidy the garage and polish the Chev. No stone was left unturned. Our house would be warm and welcoming – a place Sister could be proud of. After all, she had been abroad!

It was on the following Saturday that Mum dropped the big bomb! She arrived home with her arms full of wallpaper. Sister's room was to be painted and papered. She couldn't possibly be expected to live in it as it was.

There was only one problem. Since Sister had gone overseas, I had taken over her room. Not immediately of course. But after a suitable period it had been decided that I needed the extra space. After all, I was in high school now. There were exams to be studied for, and my own room –

more an enclosed verandah than a room – was too small even for a desk.

Until then, I'd done my homework at the kitchen table, moving every time the space was needed.

So Sister's room became mine, and her things were moved into my old one which was re-carpeted and painted in anticipation of her eventual return.

At first, when Mum spoke about Sister's room, I hoped that she was talking about my old room, though in my heart I knew differently. She had avoided mentioning it until now, allowing me to think that the current situation might be permanent.

Even so, I might have accepted the matter without complaint had not Dad responded in a way which, for him, was entirely uncharacteristic.

"What's wrong with her room the way it is?" he asked, looking over the top of his newspaper. "It's been painted and carpeted hasn't it?"

Mother looked aghast! "You don't really expect her to sleep in Howard's room do you?" was her indignant retort.

"I don't see why not," said Dad. "I thought that was understood. The lad needs the extra room for his studies and, knowing Sis, she won't be here often enough to worry."

"But she'll be bringing things back from abroad. She'll need the storage space," said Mum, clearly thrown by this unexpected opposition.

"There's room in the hall cupboard and under the stairs," said Dad, unperturbed.

"But what about the wallpaper?" stammered Mum, seeing her plan of attack going sadly awry. "I've bought it all now."

"You'll just have to take it back," said Dad in a voice that offered no alternative, and he returned to his newspaper, indicating that in his mind at least, the matter was closed.

I was staggered. To my knowledge, Dad never openly questioned Mum's decisions, or if he did, he made only token protests, and capitulated quickly. This time, however, it was clear he was not going to change his mind. Perhaps he had anticipated the turn of events and prepared himself. Or maybe something in Mum's approach seemed particularly unfair. Whatever the reason, I felt a mixture of delight and unease – delight that my needs were being considered, and unease at the thought of the confrontation with Sister that I knew lay ahead.

The rest of the fortnight passed uneventfully. Mum appeared to accept defeat gracefully, spending much of her time making my old room look as attractive as possible, and it seemed no time at all before the great day came around.

A trip to the airport was a rare and exciting excursion. Living in the outer suburbs as we did, it involved a great deal of preparation, with Dad spending hours the night before studying the street directory and making absolutely sure that the Chev was up to the journey.

That morning we all dressed under Mum's careful direction to make sure we passed muster. Shoes were shined, hair was combed and re-combed, and suits were brushed. Mum changed her hat several times and was on the point of changing it yet again, when Dad threatened to leave without her if she didn't come that moment. Given Dad's recently established authority in the household, she obliged readily.

The trip through the suburbs was exciting, but not without drama. Mum was doing the navigating, and even though Dad had meticulously marked out the route the night before, we managed to take a wrong turn which took us miles out of our way. By the time we got back on the right track, Dad was near to boiling point and Mum was close to tears. Still, we'd allowed plenty of time, and when we finally arrived at the airport and found a parking spot, there was time to spare.

Everyone was there. It was clearly regarded as an opportunity for a gathering of the clan. Relatives of whom I had only a hazy recollection arrived for the occasion, no doubt enjoying the opportunity for a day out, and eager to see the changes that two years abroad had wrought. Cousins, looking as uncomfortable as I felt, stood awkwardly, squirming in their 'Sunday best', and petulantly kicking the toes of their freshly shined shoes on the ground.

We made our way to the observation deck where we stood straining for the first glimpse of Sister's plane. The men talked knowledgeably about the aircraft that stood on the tarmac in gleaming readiness, and the women struggled to maintain their composure in the face of a wind that threatened to tear their hats off and demolish their careful coiffures.

We kids stretched to see over the heads of the people in front, silently sharing our discomfort with raised eyebrows, barely concealed sighs and adolescent sniggers as we made as if to poke some stranger in the nether regions.

At long last, Sister's plane arrived, taxiing noisily up the runway and sending clouds of dust flying with the draught from its huge propellers. It seemed an eternity before it came to a halt, the mobile stairs were moved into place, and the doors swung open. The waiting crowd began frantic jostling for a better view as the first passengers began their descent. Excited "hullo-ing" and cries of recognition came from those who could see and eager questions such as "Are you sure?" and "What does he look like?" came from those who couldn't.

The platform was a mass of pushing, shoving bodies, with tempers fraying and elbows none too delicately employed. I was pinned between a tall gentleman who kept stepping back on me and a large bosomed lady whose over-endowment threatened to engulf me, and whose handbag kept digging into my back.

Eventually though, the crowd thinned out as people moved to take up the best positions outside customs, and we managed to get a better view. Sister was one of the last to emerge, of course. Mum had become quite distraught, in spite of reassurances, and even Dad who had maintained a laudable dignity throughout proceedings had become a little perturbed.

She had obviously gone to considerable trouble to look the part, and descended the stairs with one hand holding her hat and the other containing her billowing skirt.

We joined the others outside Customs eagerly, but our hopes for a speedy reunion were soon dashed as it became obvious that customs officials were in no hurry to complete the formalities. Minutes spent in cramped and uncomfortable conditions stretched to an hour with no sign of any passengers.

Excited and good-natured joking turned to murmurs of frustration and anger. An occasional official appeared but was unresponsive to either queries or abuse before disappearing back through the doors.

Uncle Charlie, who held a position of authority with the Department of Main Roads and was clearly not used to being kept waiting, stamped off in the direction of the enquiries counter determined to get some answers, but returned none the wiser. It was almost two hours before the first of the passengers pushed their weary way through the swinging doors, loaded with luggage.

The frustration and disappointment of the previous two hours were forgotten as waiting friends and relatives rushed to exchange tearful greetings. All the suspense and anxiety of weeks of anticipation burst forth in an out-pouring of emotion as the subjects of attention turned from one adoring relative to another in an orgy of hugging, kissing and crying.

Sis, when she arrived, was a picture. Gone was the petulant teenager who'd left two years ago – her place taken by a sophisticated young lady. It was a transformation. I thought she looked a million quid, even if she was my sister, and felt as proud as Punch.

"Hey big brother," she cried when she saw me, and held me at arm's length. "What a handsome chap you've turned into. I bet Mum's flat out keeping the girls away."

"Hi Sis," I responded, blushing. For the first time I could remember, I felt some genuine affection for her. This wasn't Sister at all. From the beautifully styled hair to the hint of an English accent, she'd changed. She radiated confidence and charm, and, one by one, we were seduced by the warmth of her attention.

Mum and Dad were proud. They basked in reflected glory. This was their little girl, and she was back. All thoughts that there might be something amiss in her unexpected return were put to rest.

She didn't have a lot of luggage – that was to follow. But what she did have was eagerly carried to the gleaming Chev, polished specially for the occasion and looking fit for royalty. On the way to the car, the reunion continued. Dozens of questions were asked and answered until it became clear that Sis was getting tired, and one by one, relatives bid a reluctant farewell.

On the way home, Sis bubbled over with conversation. What a wonderful time she'd had – the places she'd been, the people she'd met. And she had lots of questions herself. What year was I in at school now? What subjects was I doing and how was I going? Who were my favourite teachers? Had things changed much at home? Had anyone moved? It seemed the excitement and chatter were never going to end.

When we turned the corner into our street there were more surprises. Those neighbours who hadn't managed the trip to the airport had rigged up a 'Welcome Home' banner, and there was a knot of people gathered outside our house cheering and clapping as we pulled into the drive.

It was like being with a celebrity; a film star or something, and Sis handled it like she'd been born to it, making sure she spent time with each of them, and not forgetting Mum and Dad either.

Aunty Ada – not a real aunt, but a neighbour that we all regarded as one of the family – had made a 'Welcome Home' cake, a batch of scones, several plates of savoury biscuits, and some cocktail frankfurts with tomato sauce. She had set up this impromptu feast, complete with a big pot of tea, on our back verandah, "so's Mum wouldn't have to worry."

We were all delighted of course! The kids especially got stuck into it without encouragement, though Mum seemed a bit put out for some reason.

Finally Dad got everyone's attention by banging a teaspoon on a cup. There were one or two 'smart Alec' comments from up the back, but everyone quietened down for the mandatory speech. This was Dad's big opportunity, and he did it in style, thanking everyone for their attendance, saying how proud we all were to have Sis back in the fold, and especially thanking Aunty Ada for all her hard work. This last part was greeted with a round of applause and 'Hear hears", although once again I noticed that Mum was less enthusiastic than most.

Dad's speech managed to bring proceedings to a natural conclusion, with the crowd gradually dispersing in a mood of jollity. Aunty Ada immediately began to fuss around clearing up, but Mum would have none of it, pointedly and firmly refusing her assistance, until Aunty Ada reluctantly agreed to leave the cleaning to us.

"Well! Of all the nerve!" began Mum indignantly as we moved inside the house, and before Aunty Ada was quite out of earshot. "That's what I call the height of rudeness!"

"Now, now Mother," said Dad firmly. "She was only trying to help, and you must admit, it made a great occasion of it."

But Mum wasn't going to be persuaded easily. "Occasion or not," she went on, "That woman had no right to march into this house and take over as if it were her own." She was really wound up now and would have gone on and on had not something else captured our attention.

In the euphoria of Sis's arrival we had forgotten about her room. Presumably someone intended to tell her about the change in arrangements, but had forgotten to do so in the excitement. She now emerged from my room with a face like thunder. There was a deathly silence.

"What's this then?" she demanded, gesturing pointedly through the door behind her. The poised and sophisticated traveller of just a moment ago had disappeared, and in her place was the stormy sister I knew only too well.

I looked anxiously from Mum to Dad and back, hoping desperately that at least one of them was prepared for this moment. Mum looked towards Dad with a raised eyebrow and a look of self-satisfaction, and he knew that his apparent victory of a week ago had been momentary. The conviction and bravado of the previous Saturday deserted him and he shifted awkwardly from foot to foot as he sought suitable words.

"Well, I've been meaning to tell you about that, lass," he began, apologetically, "Now that Howard's at high school he needs the extra room, what with his exams and all, and we've done up his old room very nicely for you," he finished gamely.

"Howard! That brat! In my room! And me in that poky little hole," Sister fumed. "Over my dead body," she shouted. "I'd sooner stay in a pub!"

And she flounced out of the house leaving Dad and me gaping and Mum with victory all over her face.

Sister was home!

Edie
Anne Garvey

Edie was the first woman anyone had heard of to have a Marcel wave in her hair. "What do you think?" she asked the children at the pub where she worked, "Pretty smashing isn't it?"

"Wonderful," said Dorothy, but she did think it looked rather strange, like a train track running all round Edie's head. "But Edie, you have lovely hair anyway."

Dorothy admired Edie's angel blonde curls and she wasn't entirely sure the Marcel wave improved things, particularly when Edie put a net over it all,

"What are you doing?" she asked, as Edie tucked the delicate bob under its brown camouflage, "Are you going to wear that all the time now?"

"Well I haven't paid one and sixpence to have it fall out after a day!"

"Fall out?" Dorothy had heard they used strong chemicals for these permanent waves but this was alarming.

"Not fall out of my head, you goose," laughed Edie, "but the wave'll loosen if I don't hold it in place."

"But we won't see your beautiful hair," chimed little Jack with dismay.

"I shall come and show you it when I take off the net before I start in the bar every night," promised Edie, "Now, what do you children want for your tea?"

Edie was from County Durham. She had left home years before and seldom returned.

"No time, no money and they'd rather have ten bob than me any day," she sniped. She was the maid-of-all-work in the pub and of her eleven shillings a week, most went to her miner father and her large and needy family in the north east.

"Yes, I've been working for five years now," she agreed, "and I've only ever seen two bob a week out of all that time.

Without my money, mi' mother'd be on the nod the whole time."

"On the nod?" little Jack nodded his head. Edie smiled.

"She cleans and mi' dad's down the mine, but if they're on short hours, then you run up credit wi' local shop, they let you have food on tick. Next thing you know, you've got a boatload of debt and the shop closes the book on you. I can't have that happen."

Edie had started her labouring life five years before, in a great house in Northumberland as a Tweenie, a maid between the floors.

"I were thrilled to get that job," she explained as she wielded the electric iron. "Living away from home, my own bed. More fool me. I soon got over that. It was murder, fourteen hours a day they had me running up and down them stairs. If I'd had a harness they'd have ridden on me back. As it was I was doing a donkey out of a job."

She only stayed so long because of her boyfriend. "But for him I'd 've been long gone, I can tell you."

"So you were going to marry him?" Dorothy asked, privately very glad Edie had done no such thing.

"Oh yes, we were stepping out together. Mind you, only on Sundays and I had to be back in uniform to serve the dinner."

Her beau, Jim, was a farm labourer. "And that was the heart of it," Edie recalled. "Every year all the workers had to face the Hiring Fair. It meant standing outside the pub where the farmers drank, waiting for work.

"I watched it once. Once and once only. That was enough for me." Edie set down her iron and leaned over the board to gaze down at Jack and Dorothy.

"When the farmers'd had a good lunch and an afternoon on the ale, they came out at last to pick out workers for the next season. They looked over the workers like they were animals. I've never seen ought like it. They chose the girls first of course, there they were, standing out like prize cows. Then the lads. My Jim was hired fast enough. He was a big fella and he caused no trouble. He soon had a red feather in his cap. That's to show you were taken... but I looked over at his dad, no one wanted him. He went home cast down. Later Jim told me the family couldn't stay on in their cottage. What a way to end."

Edie banged the iron down then resumed the pressing with indignant vigour - she was used to a heated flat iron.

"So did you finish with Jim?" Asked six year old Jack, gazing at Edie, the lost prize.

She looked up, "After that, love, I had to. I couldn't have borne it. It's hard enough a miner's daughter, but to be turned out of your home, oh no."

Dorothy was in awe of such a life of work adventure.

"And this is far and away the best job I've ever had, your mother, she is a real lady. And your father is kind and fair. You should meet mine. On second thoughts don't. Friday nights he gets drunk. Saturday night he treats his friends to drinks all round and if his dinner's not on t' table when he comes home, he's not above taking his belt to us girls, mi mother too."

Edie's blue eyes filled with tears any time she mentioned her mother, it was the only thing that stopped her sunny nature from shining through the willing day-long toil of cleaning, washing and serving.

Dorothy was proud that Edie liked her own parents so much, but the idea it was an easy job struck her as nothing less than incredible. "I don't know how you can do that," she murmured as Edie struggled on Monday morning with the beginning of the washing. They were in the stone washhouse with a monster pile of dirty clothes.

Edie collected cakes of wood shavings soaked in paraffin, then the firewood. "Just hand mi' that lighted spill," she asked Dorothy as she bent down to ignite the kindling under the massive iron-set pot full of cold water. The flames below the enormous bulb flickered and died. Edie, her face covered with black smuts from the stubborn spitting half-fire, had no option to but to clear out the guttered remains of the first attempt and restart it with a new one.

"Give us the bellows," she called, but by the time Dorothy had run over with them the fire was out. Now red in the face, Edie began again. She swore - words that Dorothy had never heard in her life poured into the smoky air. Dorothy could quite see why.

The fire alight, "Third time lucky for me," called Edie, still cheerful, she dragged over three large wooden tubs and the ladling can. Then, when the water hot was enough, she spooned it in, lowered the clothes into the boiling water and pressed the crude wooden possers up and down to work up a lather and bang out the dirt. Then she heaved up the tangle of sodden washing and manoeuvred it through a heavy iron mangle,

"I'm near out of puff this morning," she called to Dorothy "Let's both lean on this turn bar." They heaved together. Dorothy knew it was Edie who hefted the handle hardest. One entire revolution only turned the wheel two inches.

"It's that low-geared," announced Edie, "you're at it till dinner time."

Once wrung out, she dunked the whole lot back in the next tub of waiting water for starching. The whites were done. There were still the coloured clothes to wash.

Dorothy wondered how Edie could stand it.

"Walter Walter, take me to the altar," sang Edie merrily, as Dorothy went back to learning geometry. "You do that lass," encouraged Edie , calling after her. "You're a proper little scholar you are and your parents will be proud o' you."

"Don't you need a lie down Edie?" asked Dorothy preparing to vacate the washhouse "or a bath or something after all that?"

"Nay," Edie was alarmed at the idea. "I'm not paid to lie about, and any road up, I'm not having another steamy bath –

ever. I'm paying one and sixpence a week for this here Marcel wave and the steam'd take it out before you could say Jack Robinson."

"Even with a hair net?"

"Even then."

Dorothy, wondering to herself how the Marcel wave survived the laundry process in the washhouse, admired this firmness of purpose.

Edie sang as she went round the pub, one long full throated number after another. "I'm forever blowing bubbles, pretty bubbles in the air", "Margie, I think the world about you Margie, I'm always dreaming of you, don't forget your promise to me", and her favourite from the Ziegfeld Follies "Second Hand Rose". Dorothy rather wished she wouldn't sing Second Hand Rose, Edie's clothes were all given to her by Dorothy's mother, "I never get a single thing that's new," she trilled in her sweet light voice. She skilfully re-sewed them on her afternoon off, to a perfect fit for her slim body, and the rest she sent back to County Durham.

"This will do our Jamie a treat if she gets it before mi' dad or it'll be down the pawn shop and t' money down his throat," she told the children as she wrapped another parcel of Jack's little suits, destined for Pityme.

Edie was open about her ambition. "All I want," she declared, "is a home of my own. My own sheets, my own bed, my own chairs, my own front door. I should make someone a good wife, I've had enough practice looking after other folk. God knows."

In the evenings, she served behind the bar.

"Those customers in the Snug are the giddy limit," she cried one night, coming through the swing door in a fury. "I don't mind having my bottom pinched, but it's the squeezers I can't abide. They take a big handful and twist it, they get their fingers in there and…" she saw Dorothy in the corner of the licensed kitchen eating her tea and censored the rest but added, "and the Snug is meant to be for the better class of customer. That there solicitor, he's the worst. I'll bet he tells his wife he's been so busy and that's why he's late – when the only thing he's done all evening is me."

Two years later Edie fell in love. Edward came into her life as a Jug and Bottle customer and she fell for him completely. No one, not the pub customers, nor the landlady and her husband and least of all Dorothy and little Jack could see why she liked him at all.

"He's so thin," moaned Dorothy, "Edie needs someone big and strong."

"And he's so fussy," echoed Jack, " He's always picking little bits off his suit."

"Edward, Edward that's all she wants to talk about now."

"It's Mrs Mulhollands's fault," ventured Dorothy.

"How do you work that out?" her mother was curious.

"She saw him in the tea leaves. I heard her telling Edie her fortune after she'd helped do the ironing. They sat down by the fire and had a cup of tea and Mrs. Mullholland said a dark handsome stranger would walk into her life."

"But he's not dark," objected Jack.

"Mrs Mullholland says that doesn't matter, she probably didn't read the tea leaves right but she knows that Edward - well, it's him."

"And does Edie believe this?"

"She started laughing out loud when Mrs. Mullholland had finished her fortune but she paid her shilling even so," replied Dorothy.

Edie did love Edward.

"Have you ever seen such a handsome face on a man?" she asked a doubtful audience of Royal customers. "He has a right educated air, don't you think?"

Edward was in insurance. He wore a pin-striped suit and his shoes were so well polished "you could see your face in his toe caps" remarked Edie with delight. He sat with a detached and indifferent air in the Snug every Friday, whilst Edie, her cheeks toned with Tokalon powder and a coat of cream rouge on her lips, glowed with pleasure at his very presence.

"You think he's special don't you Dorothy?" she asked one evening.

"Well, he seems rather quiet," Dorothy ventured.

"That's it," Edie sighed, "He's much more refined than me."

"So are you going to marry him?" asked Jack eating his boiled egg by the fire.

Edie bent over the children. Dorothy blushed.

"We're going out, every week. And if his mother gets more used to the idea, of him, you know, getting together with a barmaid, well, I reckon one of those little cottages by Bank Dam would suit me down to the ground. One up one down they may be, but they're your own aren't they?"

"But is that what he wants, Edie? He doesn't seem as keen as you."

Jack always went one question too far, Dorothy thought. She squirmed when he asked but Edie was unfazed.

"You are right kid," she said "But then, it's a lot to ask of a fella, to look after you all your life isn't it?"

This satisfied Jack but Dorothy felt uneasy. Dear lovely Edie, with that quiet chap.

It wasn't just that she'd leave them and there would be no more songs as she served up her over-buttered toasted teacakes. Dorothy just couldn't imagine them together.

Then one Friday night Edward didn't come into the pub. Dorothy caught sight of Edie's stricken face, pale behind the Tokalon powder and knew straightaway he was missing. She started to watch the heavy swing doors. They opened and shut but no Edward entered.

Edie served the drinks stoically, her small pretty face grew stiff with disbelief. She cleared the bar in her usual way, wiped the tables and retired to her room. In the night,

193

Dorothy heard her crying into her pillow, a low muffled despairing noise that went on and on. Dorothy had to stuff her own ears with the blankets. It was unbearable. There was no outing with Edward on Sunday and the next Friday he failed to come in.

Edie was devastated.

"Don't worry Edie, you're too good for 'im," called the customers who all knew about the jilting. "Plenty more fish in the sea."

There was worse to come.

One night two weeks later, Dorothy woke to the sound of running feet outside her door. She came on to the landing to see her father putting his long Harris Tweed coat on over his pyjamas and tying his shoes laces.

"Go back to bed," he told her, "Edie needs the doctor and I'm going for him. There's nothing to worry about."

Dorothy knew there was.

Doctor Spencer came ten minutes later. She came to the top of the balustrade so she could hear him talking to her parents in the hall below.

"It's as you thought," he told them, "Edie has been to see a woman who helps girls in this kind of trouble and I'm afraid she's going to be quite ill for some weeks."

"Will she be all right - in time?" asked Dorothy's mother anxiously.

"Oh yes," Doctor Spencer was on his way out. "I see this kind of thing all the time I'm afraid. No sign of the young man involved? No, I thought not, a girl like her would never have done this unless she was, well, in despair."

Edie did return to work after two weeks in bed. She pulled the pints and made the meals but she wasn't allowed to grapple with the Monday wash any more. Mrs. Mulholland now had to do that now, as well as the finishing. There was never any time now for tea leaf fortunes by the fire. And merry Edie had gone. She did her work and served the family but her eyes were no longer flashing with the old humour.

There were no more songs and tales. The weekly visits for the Marcel wave stopped and her hair lost its dips and hollows and hung as before to her stooping shoulders.

It was on a July night that Edward came back into the pub. He walked through the heavy swing doors as if he had never been away. Edie took one look at him and left the bar to serve in the Concert Rooms. Then she came back and into the Snug to take orders. She refused to speak to him. Dorothy, intrigued by his audacious return, skulked around to see what Edie would do.

"My mother," he began, "she wouldn't let me come here. I had to try and…" but Edie had turned her head away and was walking away towards the Market Rooms.

Good, thought Dorothy

But later the next week she caught sight of Edward and Edie leaning against the wall of the side passage of the pub. He was talking earnestly to her.

"If I'd known about it," he was saying, "You didn't let me know."

The new pale silent Edie didn't reply. Dorothy saw her walk off.

"Say you'll think about it at least," Edward called after her.

And two days later she showed the family her engagement ring.

"I thought you said you never wanted to see him ever again," chirped little Jack.

"Quiet Jack, Edie is very happy."

"Nay, don't chide him," smiled Edie. "I did say that. But pride comes dear, and honestly," her large blue eyes shone, "he's all I've ever wanted," adding with all her old verve, "we're getting a cottage, just the two of us."

Anne Garvey

Anne Garvey is a journalist who has featured in the Guardian, The Times, and The Mail on Sunday. Magazines from the widely-published glossy newsstand productions to small-scale niche publications remain a constant draw for her articles.

Anne is a keen reviewer of jazz and classical music, plays and operas and once even hosted her own show on the short lived Café Radio. She is anchored in Cambridge and loves East Anglia.

Pink Leather
Dave Pescod

All three of you take deep breaths before getting out of the car. Your daughter and son pick the bags out of the boot, then walk you towards the home. You look down at the leaves stuck to the pavement like old stamps losing their colour. The big house has a white gable end with a stained glass window that gives it the look of a chapel. You remember the psychiatric ward you were in last week, the echoing screams and the smell of stale food. This home can't possibly be as bad as that, can it? In the top window a grey face peeps from behind the curtain, and you step out as fast as you can along the tree-lined street. Those walks with the dogs have kept you fit, and being an actress has played its part. Your daughter curses, but your son drops the bag and chases after you. The last light makes your pink leather coat luminescent, an odd uniform for an old resistance fighter. You hold your chin up and try to walk faster, to brace yourself for battle.

He tails you through the winding avenues, but your daughter has returned to the car to mull things over, biting her nails as she waits to face the proprietor of the home. You hear his shoes tutting and scraping on the uneven pavement behind you. The houses get grander with iron gates and security alarms. You walk for twenty minutes before beginning to tire and then you are lost.

"Stop Mum, for Christ's sake, you've made your point," your son shouts. You pause at the corner, leaning on a wooden fence. He approaches you and grips your arm.

"Leave me alone," you shriek.

"Mum, I don't want to use force, but if I have to I will." He looks to the sky seeking guidance, then turns and peers into your eyes. His voice is soft but nervous. "Why don't you just walk back with me slowly? We can talk about it." He pulls at your arm, but you grip the fence.

A man with a Labrador passes, his dog smells your feet, blowing grey air out through its nostrils.

"Are you all right?" The man asks.

By now your son is holding his head in his hands. You could pretend to be homeless, and you are. It's their idea to put you in a home. You want to tell the man everything.

"He won't leave me alone," you say. The old man stares at your son.

"She's my mother, everything's under control," he declares.

"Lies," you shout.

The old man shakes his head and leaves, unwilling to get involved in a domestic dispute. The Labrador is more curious and stays sniffing your son before the man retrieves him. You imagine he comes from a normal family with no complications, where things are easier. A family who would never be seen on the street in the Home Counties dragging a loved one into a home. But it's not as simple as that, is it? You sent your children away to school and they hated it. They've told you many times. You can't expect them to show pity or remorse for an aging loved one. Your son grabs you again. You grit your teeth and stand strong. You remember the newspaper article that stated seventy per cent of violence is domestic. There are no words spoken as he uses both arms and pulls harder.

You hang on to the fence until it becomes dislodged and a panel collapses, then another one, until you have left your mark on the suburban street. Broken wood litters the pavement and your son curses with his arms held up to the sky. He grabs your elbows, and your feet leave the ground for a few yards. You scream and drag your shoes, just like he did as a child, rubbing the leather on the rough paving slabs. He asks you to stop it, but doesn't try to bribe you with treats or rewards. For a moment you are back in Woolworths in Chorley Wood, pulling your son from the confectionery counter while he feigns dead, then kicks out in a tantrum, beating the sawdust floor in his new coat. You copy him now, and slump on to the wet leaves, rolling into a ball. You cry into your coat, and he uses bad language, stamping the pavement around you. You remember when you got him outside Woolies and pushed him into the pram, then slapped him hard. You cower, as he grabs you by the collar and drags you along Mapelthorpe Avenue, past the ornate house signs for Cedar View and Cumberland House. You pretend he has hurt you, and grasp your ankle. He crouches down next to you.

"I know why you're doing this, Mum, and I don't blame you. But you wouldn't feed yourself in the old house, this way someone will look after you." He pleads, and tries to pull you up, but you yell that your ankle is broken. You delay the return by limping and moaning.

Your daughter has gone inside to charm the owners in the hope that all is not lost, that your escape has not jeopardised their plans. Nearer the home your son relaxes his grip.

"It would mean a lot to me Mum, if you would just walk up the drive to the house. Would you do that?" he asks, trying to make eye contact, but you resist. You look up into the window and see several faces. They are not grey, their eyes are sparkling as they look down, one waves while another holds her clenched fists to her mouth. You smile at them, side step your son and push past him up the street. He doesn't follow you but curses, and takes slow steps back to the home across the shingle. Your admirers cheer you on from the window.

You step out with new-found energy and look inside the affluent homes, at children in the warm glow of television and old couples reading by lamplight. The trees rock in the wind dropping the last golden leaves onto your path. You're not sure where you're going but every step brings hope and a sense of freedom. You are six again, refusing to go home, desperate to be out on the street playing. You smooth your coat, and wet your finger to remove a stain on the pink leather. An old man raises his hat and you rush by, unsure of his intentions. There are lights at the end of the street with shops and a zebra crossing. You look for a café and try to decide on what sort of omelette you'll have, or a scone, that would go down nicely with blackcurrant jam. You cross the road and look inside the interior design shops and the estate agents but there are no cafes.

You keep walking and imagine your children back at the home sat next to each other on a sofa drinking tea from porcelain cups. They daren't ask the question, if you will still be welcome in the home, a troublesome rebel. They sip their Earl Gray nervously and listen to the whispers in the corridor as your notoriety spreads. They both stare at the carpet measuring its symmetry of wall-to-wall roses. But time is running out as they put their cups and saucers back on the silver tray, and thank the proprietors for their kindness. They leave the warmth of the house and walk to the car in silence.

By now you are in the park, sitting on a bench eating chocolate and wondering if you will stay out all night. Perhaps you'll get a bus to London and look up some old friends, some of them are bound to be in. Your best friend Pat will be pouring her sherry by the fireside. She'll let you stay for a few days till things blow over. The chocolate has all gone, and you wipe your lips with your hankie.

A man in a uniform walks up the footpath. "Mrs Scofield?" He asks.

You stare straight ahead.

"We've been looking for you." He takes his cap off and sits next to you on the bench. His walkie-talkie sends strange messages out into the night.

"It's a bit chilly to be in the park. It's nice and cosy in the car." He holds his hand out and you take it, warm and friendly. You walk slowly across the grass leaving a trail in the dew.

"Can you take me to Pat's?" you ask, but he doesn't answer. "It's not far, she'll be expecting me."

When you come out of the park gates your children are waiting by the police car. The policeman tightens his grip.

You want to get in the squad car and go to Pat's, but he takes you to them. You ignore him as he says goodbye.

The journey is made in utter silence and when you approach the home, your daughter parks as near to the door as she can. The faces sneer at them from the top window, but your children don't notice.

The proprietor opens the door and welcomes you.

"I'm awfully sorry if you've been waiting for me. I had to get some things from the shops." You stand tall and watch your son roll his eyes.

"Of course," the proprietor says.

His wife leads you upstairs to a room at the top. It's in the eaves with a view across the street and the beech trees. You don't really hear what she says, but have a desperate sinking feeling. You want her to leave you alone, though that is what you fear most, solitude. The room is small and unloved with chipped paintwork, but the radiator is hot. It could be worse.

"Supper will be in half an hour. Just call if there's anything you want." You hang your coat on the back of the door and leave your case by the bed. You switch the light off and stand by the window staring out across the roofs. Eventually your daughter and son come out and you watch them get into the car, in the same way they watched you at the school in Sussex, wondering if you would ever return. They are arguing, like you did with your husband trying to transfer blame. They'll be back in London in no time, lost in the crowds, anonymous and busy.

You hear the creak of the stairs as others go down for supper and you dread joining them. You take your coat off the hangar and turn it inside out, with the torn grey lining exposed. It will stop the sunlight reaching the skin and spoiling the pink leather.

Dave Pescod

Dave Pescod studied printmaking at the Royal College of Art in London but has always written, starting with jokes for TV and radio. In 2006 he was awarded a mentor under a Royal Literary Fund scheme and began writing prose. Since then he has written short film scripts, a stage play and had short stories broadcast on BBC Radio 4.

His stories have been published in Dreamcatcher, Transmission, Bridport Anthology, Grist and other magazines. He was awarded an Arts Council Award in 2010 to complete his first novel. His first collection of short stories *All Embracing* was published by Route in 2012.

Where the Heart Is
Tom Wiseman

An Englishman's Home

The Knight stood in the ruins of the castle, high on the cliff top, the birthplace of the legendary King. The white surf pounded the rocks below and he contemplated all that had come to pass. The faintest of memories came swirling out of the mist of time and yet some stilled moments remained captured forever in his mind. These ruins were like the remnant of a past life. These were perhaps his earliest memories, distant and hazy now as the very cliffs themselves: stood beside his mother on this very turf, the dark mouth of the cave in the opposite cliff drinking in the green sea only to let it spill out again from its slack and jagged jaw; standing with a girl on the cliff top, looking out to sea and seeing a whale break the surface; the square of stones, what was left of a cottage on the edge of the cliff, together they had learned to fly from the cliff top and swoop down over the sea.

These memories reached out from the past and into the present, touching the heart of the knight who had lived them. His feet too were moved by a yearning to revisit this sacred place. His entire being moved to bring about this return to his native land. Now he stood on the cliff top at the southern tip of the country and looked back towards the interior of the mystic green isle as it rose from the sea floor. The coastline, visible in parts through the mist, held many secret places in its twists and jagged coves, in its secluded beaches where one could make land unseen and where dark caves lead to darker tunnels beneath the earth.

The Knight had finally returned to these shores after many years abroad. He'd left as a boy seeking the road to adventure and had travelled far and wide - across scorching deserts, and through sweltering jungles, and far along the pilgrim's trail. Alive with every step, he'd met people from many walks of life with whom he had conversed in foreign tongues. He'd meditated with wise men but it was with the children that he had re-learned something of the secrets of the earth. He'd found love and passion in faraway places and his heart beat with every drop of it.

He would need it all now if his quest was to succeed.

He had called many places 'home' and many people 'family' but his pilgrimage now, a spiritual mission, brought him back to the very first of all of these.

A re-turn, certainly, but he was not visiting the same place or the same people. The Knight was not the same boy who had set out from here so long ago; though he was standing on the same spot of earth, he was at a very different point on the path.

Below him, the tide was high, in a matter of hours it would be well on its way out. For sure, the next day it would be back, but would it wash over the same grains of sand? Those glassy grains, shaped and formed by every contact with the green salt water of the sea.

The Moon hauls the world's oceans to and fro as it makes its orbit of the Earth; in turn the earth orbits the Sun, the central star of our solar system out in the arm of our galaxy as it circles other galaxies in the great cycle of the cosmos.

In the land of Kemet the people believed the Nile River to be a sacred reflection of the heavens on earth. The souls of the dead swam along this river in the sky as they returned to the source.

The particles scatter and again come together, and approach and recede – The Ship of Theseus couldn't sail the same waters twice.

The cycles and spirals of time weave their rich pattern across the fabric of life. The Knight was determined to grasp his destiny.

Of the people that he had left behind, some had grown closer, and some had grown further apart. He knew their lives were part of his mission. There had been much suffering in his native land but spring was soon to come and bring an end to this long winter. The time was right to close the chapters in need of closing in order for new ones to be opened and new cycles to begin.

The cycle of the generations was in constant flux, and the consequences of every action reached far across the incarnations. The Knight knew the time had come for him to step up and take charge of his kingdom. He would not hide away from the responsibility, he had been called and he was ready to answer that call. In his mind's eye he saw his wife and child in that foreign land far across the sea. He was ready to be a king but he knew that to be a true king he must be a humble servant. He would be in need of guidance from a higher authority and for this he sought the King of Kings.

Below him on the rocks was the figure of a fisherman looking to take a morning catch back to the tiny village.

The House of God

His lungs gasped for air and his heart beat hard as he climbed the steep and roughly hewn steps, the voyage had been long and hard and he was happy for the chance to move his limbs and breathe the smell of the soft, damp earth.

The path led to a church which stood alone on the cliff top. Although it had stood there for many centuries the Knight himself had never known the place. He had seen its outline silhouetted against the darkness as he had reached the lodging house the previous night, but now its sturdy body was revealed.

"The worshippers who braved this path come all weathers must surely be dedicated", he murmured as he climbed, but the words were taken up by the wind and reached no ears.

Once or twice his mind wandered from his purpose and he slipped or tripped on a rock. He focused and stepped onwards.

Thoughts were but autumn leaves rustling across an infinite sky. The Knight stuck faithfully to his path.

He thought of the church he'd helped build somewhere out there across the sea, not a building of stone and mortar but a living church, a family of worshippers gathered in the glory of His name. He had founded it with his great friend, a man much learned in the scriptures. This man had taught him many things and many hours they had studied and prayed together. With every understanding, the burden became less. Not that books and ink in the candlelight were the only means to the end; they were, however, an aid to the process itself, a way to remember for those who had allowed it to become forgotten.

He walked through the graveyard and entered the church. The hand-written sign in the entrance read *Welcome to our humble church. Please feel free to explore it as you wish, nowhere is out of bounds in the house of God. St. Materiana's chapel may be used for private prayer.*

The Spirit was alive here, he could tell. A spirit found in the ways and actions of the people, not in the cool and reverend smell of old stone as many mistakenly believed.

He passed through the unlocked door and found himself stood in the house built for education and worship. He was met by St. George himself, the Palestinian patron, depicted in the beautiful stained glass of the nave window; a suitable encounter on the very day on which he was celebrated throughout the land. The Knight knew how to read the signs.

Psalm 86: Ye are gods.

For those that chose to be.

He was getting closer. Harmony was all that The Knight desired.

He eased open the door of the chapel and stepped inside.

A bench opposite a small altar and a notebook, the Knight walked over and examined the words at the very top of a fresh new page: *Dear Lord, deliver our family from the tormentor.*

The heavens reflected in the Earth. The very prayer he had held in his heart as he had climbed the path and knocked on the door to ask was there to meet him.

Kingdom Come

Home is where the heart is. Where your treasure is, there your heart will be also.

Only God knows what is written in a man's heart.

I am my brother's keeper.

Back on the cliff top the Knight's heart sang with gratitude in the salty air. He listened to the wind and the occasional cry of a gull. He gazed across the sea and for a moment he felt his wings spread and soar towards freedom across the horizon. The smell of the green earth filled his nostrils and he was back on the rocks. All that he had born witness to had confirmed that he was on the right path and he breathed a sigh of contentment.

He had set out to experience the world, to live and to love and to evolve as part of the great process. The tides may turn and turn again but there was one great current which it was futile to swim against. The worlds were at war but the Knight carried peace in his heart; he knew he must fight for the path of the light and, eventually, return to the source. For now though the journey continued. He was the sovereign ruler of his dominion and he knew he would serve it well, a humble warrior who could rely on many brothers-in-arms.

He would need them, the Knight knew, in the many battles that awaited him on the long journey home.

Tom Wiseman

Tom Wiseman was born in Oxford, England. A writer, rapper and English teacher, he is passionate about travelling the world and sharing his experiences through his art. He currently lives and teaches in Mexico.

A Commission
Tim Futter

The middle-aged man stepped out of his car. He closed the door and the light flashed as it locked. Standing on the pavement he looked up at the property, his clipboard and pen in hand. He walked along the hedge of the large corner plot. As he entered the driveway he felt his foot sink into the deep gravel. The crunching sound was reassuringly expensive. The man stopped and straightened his tie. He was glad he was wearing his best suit. He climbed the three steps up to the very grand entrance and pulled the old fashioned bell that was set in the wall. Ding Dong. Even the sound of the bell spoke money. The door opened.

"Ah, good morning. Mitchell's the name. Mitchell's Estate Agents. Miss Phillips I presume?"

"No. I'm Miss Phillips' secretary. Please come in."

Mitchell entered the hall. He cast a professional eye around, noting the five white panelled doors and the wide staircase with its white banister rail. Above was an imposing chandelier. He made a note to ask about the fixtures and fittings being included in the sale. Miss Phillips' secretary opened a door.

"Would you wait in the drawing room please? I'll let Miss Phillips know you are here."

"Thank you."

The drawing room was equally magnificent. The furniture like the house was late Victorian. The glass-fronted bookcases held leather bound volumes. Mitchell walked to the French windows and looked out to the garden. The bright sunshine shone through the trees. Mitchell made a mental note, he would try and get prospective buyers to view as quickly as possible. The summer weather showed the property off to its best advantage.

"Mr Mitchell. How kind of you to have come round so quickly. I'm very pleased to meet you." They shook hands. Her manner was businesslike.

"Miss Phillips. I'm more than happy to be prompt. This is exactly the type of property we like to have on our books. In all honesty I was anxious to secure your instructions."

"Have no fear Mr Mitchell. I will be using your firm and you will be the sole agents."

"That's very kind of you, we will be more than happy to act for you, Miss Phillips."

"It's not quite as simple as that. I have some very specific requirements. Forgive me, where are my manners. Tea. Mr Mitchell?" It was more of an instruction that a question. Without waiting for a reply she pulled on a plaited silk cord hanging from the ceiling. "I see you were admiring the garden. Shall we take tea on the lawn?"

"Allow me." Mitchell opened the glass doors. He stepped back to let Miss Phillips lead the way.

They walked to a cast-iron garden table and sat in the matching chairs.

"This is a wonderful garden you have here."

"Yes, I suppose it is, I seldom come out here. Roberts takes care of it all. I must say it's very nice having fresh flowers in the house. Forgive me Mr Mitchell, but what are you smiling about?"

"Oh I'm sorry, it's just that… well I find it hard to believe that you don't use the garden very often. It's such a beautiful spot and… well it's more than that. I have a confession to make to you. You see, I know this garden. I know this garden very well indeed."

"You do? How so? You can't possibly know this garden. I am a good few years your senior and I have lived here all my life."

"Let me explain. When I was a young boy I used to climb onto the top of that wall at the bottom of the garden. In those days there was a high hedge on this side of the wall and from my vantage point I could see into the garden."

"That's quite correct, there was an high hedge in those days."

"Presumably to keep out prying eyes." Mitchell allowed himself a smile. Miss Phillips smiled back.

"What peculiar creatures children are. Why on earth would you want to look at this garden?"

"Well, for me it was a magical place. It was the most beautiful place I had ever seen. I suppose I dreamed of living in such a grand house, with such a beautiful garden. I used to climb up there and look at it, dreaming of the kind of life I would lead in such a place. It reminded me of the kind of place one read about in story books, a sort of fantasy land. And if I'm really honest with you, it still is the kind of image I think of when I think of what might be a perfect life."

"That's incredible. I can hardly believe my ears."

"It's true I can assure you. I mean to say, it must have been wonderful for you, living here. You must be terribly sad to be selling the place."

Miss Phillips laughed. She could not control herself. It was a polite laugh, but she could not stop. The tears ran down her face. Mitchell leaned forward anxiously, unsure of what to say. He was relieved when Miss Phillips' secretary arrived with a tea tray. The secretary looked at Miss Phillips and then proceeded to pour the tea. The tea service was of the finest bone china. Mitchell picked up his cup and saucer and stirred his tea. He was relieved to have something to do.

"Thank you."

"Your very welcome, Mr Mitchell."

The secretary walked back into the house. Falteringly Miss Phillips began to regain her composure. Sobs of laughter interrupting her every time she attempted to speak.

"Forgive me, Mr Mitchell. I must explain. You see the truth of it is, I hate it here and I always have done. I can't stand the place and now that I have inherited it, I can't wait to get rid of the damn place. As a child I hated it, always being looked after by nannies, and later on by housekeepers, I just hated it. It was such a relief when I went off to boarding school. So much better than living here in this cold old mausoleum with everything immaculate and in its place. And the Nannies, the strict Nannies, with their rules and regulations. It was stifling, truly stifling. There's no other word for it. I have hated every minute that I have spent in this house. It was like a prison then and it has been like a prison ever since. I can't wait to get rid of it. With your help Mr Mitchell."

"Er, of course, er…forgive me. It's just that, well, it's a bit ironic, me dreaming of living here and you hating every minute of it."

"My dear Mr Mitchell, you haven't heard the funniest part. Just wait until I tell you of the specific requirements that I spoke of earlier. I have had my solicitors do some research for me, and that is why I have chosen your firm to handle the sale. I will be requiring somewhere to live and I understand that your firm are the letting agents for the old warehouse buildings at Clinkers Yard."

"Yes that's correct. We do act for the landlords of that property. But I don't understand, why are you interested in that?"

"Because, Mr Mitchell, I intend to live in one of the flats above the warehouses. To be precise I would like to live in the end flat that backs onto the old lock-ups to the rear of the property."

"You can't live there, nobody has lived there for years. It's a complete wreck of a place."

"I will pay for all the renovation work and whatever rent the landlord may require."

"But you can't be serious. It makes no sense, you can't move from here to that old slum."

"That's exactly what I am going to do, and I shall rely upon you to arrange it for me."

"But it hasn't got a front door, at least, not one of its own. It shares the entrance with the warehouse below. You have to walk through the warehouse to reach the entrance door."

"I know. I propose a fire escape that follows the route from the Dormer window in the roof and the slope of the roof down to the back wall, to the yard outside the lock ups. Do you understand where I mean?"

"Yes. I know it like the back of my hand, but why?"

"Because it always looked so exciting. You see when I was a young girl I used to watch a little boy jump out of that window and run across the rooftops and down onto the back wall and then swing on the metal pole with the T.V. aerial. He used it like a fireman's pole, spinning down to the ground.

"It was the most exciting thing I ever saw. A young child running free. That image has never left me. I have always dreamed of living such a free existence. So you see we all have childhood dreams that have to be pursued."

Tim Futter

Tim Futter was born and brought up in Cambridge where he studied A-levels at Cambridge College of Arts and Technology. He later studied English and American Literature at the UEA in Norwich.

When he returned to Cambridge in later life Tim wrote a few pieces for FLACK magazine for the homeless. Emboldened by seeing his work in print he started his MA in Creative Writing at his old Alma Mater – now Anglia Ruskin University – which he will complete in 2014.

Searching For Point Home
Alex Ayling

There's a lot of problems with living in a big city, but being mugged was one I never paid much attention to.

As I lay on the side of the pavement, the cool wet concrete pressed hard up against my face, I decided it was time to move that further up my list of things to look out for, and more importantly, it was time to leave the big city.

My eyes focused on the flickering street-light across the road, as its reflection danced around on the pavement, creating a stop motion picture around it, as moths were frozen in place for a fraction of a second before moving to a new position, as if the light could freeze time. The first splashes of rain fell onto my face, replenishing the already damp ground. I pulled myself onto my hands and knees, the blood from my mouth drooling onto the ground as I grabbed my ribs in pain at exhaling an exhausted breath.

The muggers had been particularly brutal, and having never been mugged before, my handling of the situation could have been better. Several flurries of fists and elbows and knees later, one mugger held me face down in the concrete, while the other raided my rucksack, pulling out the last of my money which hadn't been hidden down my pants in fear of being mugged. As I slipped out of consciousness, staring up at the night sky, I heard them run off, not before giving me a final couple of kicks. It was at that moment that I experienced pain. No metaphorical contemplations on life, just blinding pain, both dull and stabbing. Blacking out was truly a godsend at that point. As I recalled these earlier memories, they seemed to rush up again and I felt my brain go fuzzy, a black hazy mist covered my vision and my limbs lost all feeling, as I crumpled once more to the floor.

Waking again, face still on the side of the road, I decided the pavement had been closer to me than anyone I had met in the four months since I'd left home.

"Hello pavement, how many people will walk on you today I wonder?" The words came out in a hollow and cracked voice, so that they floated into the air sounding like a creature from a B-list horror movie. The pavement didn't respond, its cracked concrete oblivious to my question. I'd like to say I was disappointed by the lack of response, but I don't think my brain had been damaged by my attackers, so I was sure at least that I wasn't going to hear talking floors any time soon.

I rolled myself towards the wall, and sat up against the cool brick, staring at the lamp post across the street. As I watched the light flicker, and finally die, I looked towards the blue sky down the road, a cool azure blue, as the first lines of purple and orange began to peek out across the horizon of inner city London. I rested against the wall, watching my breath float towards the sky in clouds of water vapour, and I began to wonder about my return home. I had been gone so long I wasn't sure what it would be like to see their faces again, as they had only existed in my mind for the past four months.

I'd called them once, and just to let them know that I was still alive, and not being drugged up in some kind of druggie den, that I had a job (I worked on a cart which sold freshly baked cookies, which had been firebombed, as the owner had borrowed some money from some bad people, and torched his own stall for insurance money, which left me without a job, but with a 'burning' desire to stay away from cookies) and was living in a place, but declined them an address. I wasn't ready for my past coming to visit me, especially since I'd left in not the best circumstances. My parents were accommodating, far more than I thought they would be, but I couldn't not feel their sadness and worry as I said goodbye to them, as they sent me off on a wet day, the rain blurring the image of them as the coach pulled away. I shook my head clear of those memories, and tried to focus on the world around me, to stop me from looking into my mind.

I watched as the early risers in their beat-down cars drove down the road, metal boxes with their metal noises disturbing the quiet sounds of city air and birds singing, before disappearing, their engines power-housing down the road to disturb more of the sleeping air. I went to check my watch, and chuckled as I stared down at a bare wrist as I realised it was gone. I slowly moved my leg closer to me, and pulled the shoe off my foot, carefully pulling out the money I had stored in there. I counted the notes, a final one-off payment from the cookie-cart boss who'd called it severance pay after 'firing' me. He enjoyed making puns, I felt it was unnecessary.

A bus pulled leisurely in front of me, and I struggled up, brushing myself off, realising it was pretty useless, considering I'm covered in street dirt and blood. I exhaled slow and measured, as I signalled to my legs to begin moving, limply dragging them across the pavement, and a careful stepping onto the bus's crystallized grey floor. The bus driver stared, fixated on what I can only see as I turn my head to the window to gaze on my reflection, a black and red tapestry where my face used to be. I turned to the driver and motioned for a ticket, trying to smile, and hoping it didn't scare him even more.

"Yeah... ummm... long night. Can I have a ticket please?" I mumbled, trying not to open my mouth, as I wasn't exactly sure what the state of it was. My tongue felt funny, but other than that, I was trying not to think about it.

"Listen kid, I don't really think you need a ticket at this point. Perhaps a doctor is more appropriate?"

His words were not sarcastic, but filled with genuine concern, but I couldn't help but feel pissed off by them. As if perhaps I had not realised this whole mugging and being beaten was not worthy of a trip to my local A&E, or perhaps I could just sleep it off. Shaking the thoughts out of my head by shaking it, I simply repeated my request for a ticket, but he motioned for me to go through and told me it wasn't worth it for a measly £2.40. I thanked the driver, and went and sat down right next to the exit, as I began my odyssey to get home, miles away from this urban sprawl, nestled away in a small town up north, complete with post office and mildly racist but loveable villagers. My parents weren't exactly small-town people, and perhaps that was why they were more accepting and less parentally protective over me leaving, even if it wasn't under good circumstances, my exile away from the small town seemed to be less of a bombshell than I expected. I was pushing my sixteenth year, and I had made a deal with my older friend from London to live with him down there, as we had never met in person. As I rubbed my tender face, worrying about the possibility of permanent damage, I realised that perhaps city life had hit me all at once with its finest horrors.

The last two months of poverty had proved almost unbearable, had it not been for the few friends I'd made who didn't try to steal my possessions. The 'friend' who had taken me in, like a lost animal he'd given shelter to, was barely able to take care of himself, so I was in essence, thrown to the dogs of urban life. My mind almost flipped trying - and failing - to micro-manage my minimum wage to keep myself fed on cheap noodles and tea until my next pay-cheque and making sure my flat-mate didn't steal what little I had to buy drugs. And of course, when the long days were over, and on a night when there weren't people round, my safe haven lay in TV, and the varying quality of the late-night shows. It was a life not even close to the wild visions I'd imagined for myself, a tale of adventure and freedom, hard work and luck, passion and finding a home for my soul, a place of infinite mystery and knowledge, where I would find myself both constantly challenged and forever at peace.

Of course, once I'd reined in my wild imagination, even then I still imagined things would go better than this. I thought of taking a trip to a dream location, and becoming part of its cultural core. I planned to get a job, and then look for my real passion in artwork, as I began to seriously think about becoming an artist. I thought a trip to somewhere new would become a launching point, and I would meander around the snaking urban sprawl, trying to capture moments in time of London and in a sense try to bring to life a world I had only dreamed about.

So I left home, and my parents could do nothing but grudgingly accept. While they came from opposite ends of life, my father being a geologist, and my mother a nature photographer, both had a deep-rooted passion for the natural world around us, and the fragile nature of its existence. Since both had done their fair share of exploration across the world, they were actually quite considerate in meeting me halfway, and allowing me to go to London so long as I lived with a friend.

My parents were both free spirits, one fascinated with time gone by, the other fascinated with freezing time itself. My father was obsessed with the past and its consequences, often teaching me about the ground, and what lies beneath it. To look at a building, and not to marvel at it for its decoration, but for its material itself, brings things into a new light. And my mama was fiery in nature, and her photography displayed it. All around the house were scattered Polaroids, canvases, and just general photographs everywhere. Walking into a room and seeing a thousand different views from a thousand different places, only helped to ingrain a deep sense of wonder at the world around me, and naively allowed me to believe that I wanted to see all of it. Well this was the side that wasn't captured in those photographs. I closed my eyes and I could almost see the pictures at home, the vibrant blue of the Azores from a helicopter, a eagle's claws bared over a running hare, thousands of flying fish cutting their way through the air and sea, a thou-

"There's a hospital a couple of streets away from here. I suggest you go there son, you like you've had seven shades of shit beaten out of you." The driver's musical northern voice brought me out of my reminiscence of home, and I pulled myself up off the seat, flaking yellow paint collecting under my fingernails as I dug into the pole to stop from groaning with pain.

"Thanks for the free ride, sir." I noticed my accent had become slightly distorted, as my words were slurred and I had drawn out the sir, making me sound a little bit more of a Londoner. If nothing else, I would be able to bring that back with me I thought, as I eased myself off the bus and saw it drive round the corner, disappearing as leisurely as when it rolled into my view. Then I headed in the opposite direction to my house (well, really my friend's house), thinking to myself that the hospital could wait until after what I had in mind.

I walked out into the orange glow of a rising sun, the purple and blue sky now rapidly retreating away from the advancing army of colour attacking it. Walking with my head down, I began to notice the cuts on my arms, and how one of my hands was aching sorely. As a cough escaped my lungs, I felt the sharp pain, and wondered if my ribs were broken, but I limped on, my legs becoming numb as I shuffled them up flights of stairs, falling down at intervals to catch my breath and to stop myself from tumbling back down. I crawled up the last few steps, and unlocked the door to my 'home' for the last time.

It was grim. Obviously Mickey, my friend, had decided to have a party with his friends, because bodies and bottles lay strewn across a carpet full of cigarette butts, and the smell in the air definitely indicated something stronger than cheap vodka had been done. When I flung open the bathroom door, the smell of vomit and blood assaulted my nose, and I slammed it shut. So this was it, I thought to myself, this was the home I had carved out for myself in London, a dingy two-bedroom flat, complete with a druggie and a dangerous stove. I just stood in the middle of the room, not quite believing how it had come to this. The TV, my only bastion of entertainment left, had someone's foot through it.

I fell into a chair, jaw open, as the shock and terror of everything that had happened hit me, and I cried. I cried, warm tears rolling down my painful face, into a room of people who were unconscious to hear, both in mind and body, the people who destroyed things, and broke things, just because that was how they functioned. And I had fallen into them, but I wasn't one of them. I did not destroy; I wanted to build, to create. Destroying was easy I thought as I watched them party often, and watching them doing things easily helped me to see why the opposite is so hard. But now there was no musings, just pain. Pain at having things go so wrong, and the pain I was feeling in my chest.

As a drunken woman begun to stir though, I silenced my sobbing, and washed my face in the kitchen sink, the cold water cooling my tender skin, and wiping away the tears from my swollen face. I headed to my room, thankfully which I had locked, and gathered my suitcase and begun to pack my things, old clothes smelling not great, half empty toiletries, and finally, well worn art equipment. Pencils and brushes and sketchbooks and paints and all of them useless, but when combined, I could create something I liked, that I enjoyed, and what I made for others to enjoy. As I loaded my work into my suitcase, I picked up a sketch I had done specifically for Mickey. It wasn't really a sketch, more of a doodle. It had Mickey with his fist through the clock face of Big Ben, standing like a giant on Westminster Bridge as cars were frozen around his feet, his cartoon features upended in mischievous glory. I wanted to make a statement, as Mickey's eyes stared straight at me, challenging me to just try a man who can stick his fist through one of London's most famous landmarks. Pulling a pen from a drawer, I scribbled a message onto the back of the sketch:

Dear Mickey.

I hate you. Good luck living here by yourself. I just got mugged, and I might have broken bones, as well as a broken psyche. I'm going home. Don't ever try to contact me again. I hope you fix your drug habit, and your friends are arseholes.

Bye.

A final drop of blood from my arm fell onto the page, and I would have laughed at how poetic this was, but my chest was still killing me. I braved a trip into the bathroom, mouth and nose covered, and grabbed some pain-killers off the shelf and headed out of the now hazardous room. Two tablets later, I grabbed some tape out of the drawer, and taped the sketch to Mickey's face, knowing that unless he had become blind, he wouldn't miss it. Then I pulled some ham out of the fridge, and consumed an entire box. I thought of myself, broken and bruised, eating cold meat in a plastic chair in a now unrecognisable shell of a home, containing drunk strangers and broken memories of the night before, and I couldn't think about how far I had come from what I used to call home. Home as an idea was shattered for me. The idyllic setting of my parent's life was all too dreamlike for me now, a fairytale world that had no place existing in what is the real world. The real world however, can never be home to me, because I can't help but dream of greater things, of something more than 26p noodles, and bills, and late night television. My home was the journey, the intermediary points of destination A to B. The brick wall and flickering street light were my home tonight, and so was the bus journey, and everything else. My A & B are meaningless to me because they aren't there. All point A could have ever represented was I had to get to point B, and all point B ever represented was my next stop before point C. Even now as I head towards a train to get home, they're just points on a map I'm traversing and-

The ground came way too fast. My daydreaming had once again been broken by the crushing reality around me, and the

blood pounding in my ears muted out most of my pained shouting. I pulled myself up, teeth gritted, and I stared daggers back at the offending object. A spray can flat on its side. I picked it up and threw it straight at the door. The explosion of bright red as the can burst was my last memory of that place before I swung open the door and walked to the station.

I sat on the platform, the cool concrete pressing into my arms, numbing the stinging pain. I felt drained, mentally and physically. And yet I was also energised and happy, the rising sun not yet high enough to be blinding, and the buildings cutting their way across the orange background, their blocky forms steadfast against the sky, casting shadows across the streets below. I could hear the birds singing, softer now as they begun to compete with the noise of traffic. I could smell the ever-so-slight tinge of petrol in the air. I felt my senses combining to create this tapestry in front of me, an image of an urban sprawl, the smell of concrete and city air, the metallic taste of dried blood and the remnants of my last meal, the feeling of the hard ground beneath me. And in this moment, nothing felt more natural than to do what I did next. I pulled out my pad, and began to sketch the world in front of me, right from my eyes, capturing the birds frozen in flight, the towering buildings like blocks against the vibrant sun, even the rails down below hit by the sunlight.

Everything was so clear, and even though I knew this feeling could never last, I wasn't naive enough to believe this would be the only time I could see the world so clearly. I knew it would come again, though I could never really know when. Just like I could never know everything that happened to me in the last night until it happened. I thought about them, the muggers, the bus drivers, the early risers, the party goers, everyone functioning in their own special way, existing at the same time yet never even recognising the other's existence. Maybe I'd never be an artist, or truly experience a

231

cultural revolution in my mind, but right then just for that second, I could just enjoy the city for what it is.

I hear footsteps behind me, and turn the good half of my head towards him, an old spectacled man with a long beard and an incredibly sharp suit. He stands and peers over my shoulder inquisitively. I catch his gaze, and in a deep and gravelly voice, he asks me, "What is it?"

I realise he can see the pad but can't see what's on it, so I pick it up out of my lap, and pass it to him, my bruised face in full view, but he seems untroubled by it. I think he must have seen a lot worse in all his years, so I assume he isn't that bothered. I turn my head back to the vista, the light from the sun almost blinding now so that I'm squinting, and can feel the heat on my bruised skin.

"Home." I say, and a smile passes across my lips.

Alex Ayling

Alex Ayling is of Portuguese and British descent, born in Hammersmith, London, and is currently at college. He hopes to go on to study film at university, with ambitions to become a screenwriter, perhaps eventually a director.

Oxford Dogs
Linda Brucesmith

The homeless men of Oxford sit with sleet-painted shoulders. Their dogs are covered with thermal blankets – lumps with just their noses showing. The men draw on cigarettes and the smoke curls into the coats and the scarves of crowds hurrying for tall red buses and rattling trains and homes in other places. Their gazes twitch and leap. Their dogs' eyes are shut tight.

On St Giles Street, Nick Halsey's folded into the dusk and the twelfth century doorway of St Giles Church. There's a square of cardboard at his feet with please written on it in spidery, penned letters and beside it, a paper cup part filled with coins. Nick's snoring. His beanie's pulled over his forehead, his scarf's covering his chin. The sheepskin collar he's turned up hasn't been white since long before he inherited the jacket he now wears all day, most days. He's folded his arms over his chest, tucked his hands in their fingerless gloves under his armpits. The loop at the end of his Australian kelpie's leash is wrapped around his right hand. The lead trails over his stomach. The other end's clipped to the dog's collar.

Missy's half asleep – part resting, part watching. When a man pauses in front of their spot the fur over her eyes wrinkles as she looks at him – tolerant, accepting and hopeful of treats. It's a look that pulls charity.

The man studies her, then Nick. He peers into the cup. Missy raises her head. She's seen this before. She pricks her ears, listens for the chink of coin on coin.

But the man doesn't donate. Instead he crouches, shakes the loose change from the cup into his hand, closes his fist around it. He pushes the coins into the pocket of his hoodie, zips the pocket closed. He crushes the empty cup into a ball, sets it between Nick's boots.

The man turns his attention to Missy. He considers her collar, the primrose yellow fabric tied around her neck like a scarf, the lead that binds her to Nick. He reaches inside his jacket, produces a flick knife with polished wood set into its stainless steel handle. It's spring-loaded and it's got a mini torch built into it so that when the blade is revealed – curved like a razor on one side, serrated like sharks' teeth on the other – he can see exactly what he's doing. He shushes Missy as the knife clicks open. He crouches, studies the line of the lead, lifts it between two fingers and makes a loop. The knife slices cleanly through the leather.

The man gets to his feet and pats his hip. "Come," he whispers. He pulls on the cut lead. Missy creeps from the blanket, her tail tucked between her legs. Her claws scritch, scritch, scritch on the pavement as the man takes her away.

An hour later, Nick does his wake up ritual. Before he opens his eyes, before he's reminded of the things his eyes show him he likes to wind in Missy's leash and feel for her weight, his anchor in a shifting world. For Missy, the tug's as good as a whistle, as fine as the waggle of a stick before it's thrown over grass. When Nick peels his eyes open she's always there looking at him, vibrating her tail under the blanket. He says, "Hey, Miss," and scratches her head. She pushes up, into his palm.

This time, when Nick pulls on Missy's lead there's no resistance. When he looks, there's a cold space by his feet. He works himself upright. He contemplates the place where Missy should be, pulls at the leash, grasps the leather with his free hand then runs it through his palm until he's got the severed end clasped in his fist. He stares at it.

"Oh, fuck," he says. "Missy!"

He pushes himself to his feet. The balled cup skitters across the pavement as he staggers into pedestrians. He shouts and calls; people cross to the other side of the street. When he turns to gather up his blankets he sees the cup. Tears start, fat and heavy.

"Bastards," he says.

Nick does the rounds of the city's street people. He starts with the ones who have dogs. He does Cornmarket Street and he does High Street and he does the Broad Street strip that runs between The Fudge Kitchen and Balliol College, past the A-frame sign offering ghost tours for nine quid. The dog people listen and pass the story on and that night they pull their animals onto their laps and hold them close and don't sleep much.

When Nick tells Joe the fire juggler the news the next morning Joe says he'll push one of his torches – lit – up the bugger's you-know-what when they find him. Nick's eyes fill with water at that and Joe's so embarrassed by the emotion he says he's sure they'll get the dog back. No doubt about it. But he doesn't really think they will.

Nick wanders off.

Joe's so bothered he stashes his torches and does rounds of his own. He goes to the spots held by dog people and tells them they need to come with him now, to the Oxford Mail, where they'll get their picture taken – with their dogs – so the paper can publish the story and Oxonians will know to keep their eyes open.

Three hours later, Joe's got a group waiting on the pavement outside the newspaper's office. He goes in and tells the receptionist some bastard's stolen a homeless man's dog while he was sleeping and they need to get the dog back and he's got twelve people and twelve dogs outside and what did they want to do about it? The receptionist looks at Joe's soot-blackened hands and sniffs at his kerosene smell. She picks up the phone and calls the newsroom. A few minutes later a pink-cheeked girl carrying a notebook emerges from the lift.

"I'm Catherine," she extends her right hand. "You wanted to report a lost dog?"

Joe looks down at the fresh skin of Catherine's delicate fingers. When he hesitates, Catherine reaches, grasps his hand. Her skin reminds him of babies.

"Joe. Yeah," Joe says. "Nick Halsey's had his dog pinched. He'll do himself in without it. What kind of no-good steals a dog from a homeless man?"

Catherine gestures at the chairs pushed against the wall. "Will we sit down, Joe? Can I ask you some questions? Do you want a coffee?"

"Uh, yeah, sure. But this isn't about me," Joe says.

"I understand…" says Catherine.

"Look, I brought some people with me. They're outside. I'm thinking a photo would be better – you know, a picture says a thousand words and all." Joe heads for the door and Catherine follows him into the afternoon's chill.

The dog people are gathered on the footpath. Leaning and sitting. They're not talking, just waiting. When Joe and Catherine approach the dogs turn their heads. Their combined gaze is a kindly thing which makes Catherine's chest ache. One by one, their owners consider her too. Catherine pulls her mobile from her jeans pockets, calls for a photographer. The image runs front page the following morning. The paper is inundated with calls, letters to the editor from outraged Oxonians who want to provide puppies. The paper's social media feeds run hot. A London daily hears the story and decides on a follow-up.

Five days later, Nick's all snot and tears and telling anyone who'll listen he'll top himself if Missy doesn't turn up soon. "You know she pulled me out of a fire once," his face is little-boy scared. "I've had her since she was five weeks old, bottle-fed her when she was a pup. She knows me like no-one does. And she's microchipped too, you see? Means we'll find her, right?"

The following week the Oxford Mail runs an interview with Lucy the barmaid who says she met Nick four years ago when she started at the Eagle and Child pub, down the road from his spot. She'd wanted to pay her luck forward and so she'd given him a fiver. It was the only thing she had. "If I'd had coins I'd probably have used those so it wasn't anything

238

special. I put the money in his cup and he stared at me like I was a jack-in-the-box. I thought he might have been a bit simple. Then he said, sitting on the cold cement like he was, 'Are you sure?' Like my giving must be a mistake, a little kindness like that. He picked up the cup and he pushed it at me. When I said the money was for him he said, 'Bless you,' so quiet I almost missed it. I cried all the way to work."

Lucy tells the Mail how most days, after the Eagle and Child's midday rush settles, she brings Nick food. "Not slop from other people's plates," she says. "Proper bits. The boss is good like that." She says she's had him home a few times for a shower, then she blushes. "Just a shower, mind. That's all it's ever been. Missy always behaved a treat." She pauses and frowns. "I see Nick now and he just sits and stares and cries. I don't know what will happen to him if we don't find that dog."

Children read Nick's story, bring their animals for him to pet. A month after Missy's disappearance, a young mother comes by with a youngster clutching a toy cocker spaniel. "He's been pestering me," she tells Nick, who's sitting in the doorway of St Giles Church with his head at kid height. The child looks into his face. Nick knows what's coming and prays he'll keep it together. The boy's frightened but determined. "You can have Scruff because your dog got stolen," he thrusts the toy at Nick's chest. "He's my favourite." His clear blue eyes consider Nick's blanket. "He doesn't eat much."

Nick's head hurts. He's pinned between the stone wall behind him and the woman and child in front of him. The dog's caramel and white acrylic fur is soft and deep. The child looks at the dirt under Nick's fingernails. Nick says, "Thanks, little fella," and manages to keep his voice steady. "I'll look after him proper." He glances at the mother. She's looking at the child and her face is devastated and proud at the same time. He puts the toy where Missy used to sit.

Nick becomes a celebrity. People seek him out, tell him they're sorry about his dog. The ones who would have given him money before, give him more, and those who have never given anything, give something. Nick finds he now has money for shelters most nights but doesn't want to leave his spot in case Missy returns.

Spring doesn't come. It's cold. Nick doesn't eat or move around much. Oxford's dog people visit, sit beside him with their animals at their feet. They don't talk because there's nothing to say and nothing to be done.

The ghost tour people drift past every Friday at midnight when the temperature's at zero and the air's like ice. They've done the circuit of the city's old places, they're on their way back to their starting point and mostly, they're disappointed because the tour hasn't spooked them the way they'd hoped.

This particular Friday, they pass Nick's spot and a girl squeaks. The rest of the tour's passed but she wants a buzz so she's gone to take a closer look at Nick, who's toppled sideways across the steps. His head's at an awkward angle and the edge of the step's pressing into his cheek. His eyes are open. When the girl calls to the group her voice is shrill and people smile at each other because she's raised goose bumps on them and that's what they've paid for. The group leader is a young man called Silas and although he's crawled through crypts and cemeteries and out of bounds spaces in churches and cathedrals he's never seen a dead person before and he doesn't like it. Silas calls the police. The group huddles together.

Catherine reports Nick's death for the Oxford Mail.

No-one moves to take Nick's patch.

There's the feeling whoever sits in his spot should have a dog. Lowlife dog thieves shouldn't call the shots.

Two weeks after Nick's passing, Jimmy thinks enough time's gone by for him to take a look, make the move if no-one else has. He shoulders his stuff, sets off with his bulldog trotting behind. As he approaches Nick's doorway, Winston snuffles and grunts. He runs ahead, pulls at his lead.

"Wait on, fella," says Jimmy. Winston barks.

There's a skinny mutt curled into Nick's corner. When Jimmy approaches it raises its head and gazes at him – hopeful of treats. The dog's got a torn ear and there's a crusty scab over its eye. The three of them stare at each other. Winston sits.

"Shit," Jimmy tells Missy. He scratches her head. "Where in hell have you been?"

Linda Brucesmith

Linda Brucesmith is the principal of Aqua Public Relations based in Brisbane, Australia. She has worked as a journalist in Sydney, Melbourne, and on Queensland's Gold Coast. Her short fiction has been selected for publication in The Fiction Desk's 2013 Ghost Story Anthology, *Andromeda Spaceways Inflight Magazine* and *Perilous Adventures Magazine*, highly commended in the 2012 Fellowship of Australian Writers National Literary Awards and long-listed in the 2012/13 Fish Short Story Prize.